*With games like this, how would Dallas ever convince Julie of the merits of baseball?*

"It doesn't get much better than this," Dallas said as he and Julie settled down after a trip to the concession stand. "Hot dogs, Cokes, a sunny afternoon. And kids out there playing baseball."

"That was not a strike, ump," one parent yelled.

"The ump needs glasses, " another chimed in.

Julie glanced at Dallas.

He shrugged. "Sometimes the fans get a little overzealous."

A Gentry player tried to steal home and got thrown out.

"He was safe!" a mother screamed. "There was no way he was out." She started to climb down from the bleachers, but her husband held her back.

"They can't do that to us," she argued with her husband. Her son threw his helmet in the dirt...

The fans booed. Mel Cooney stood nose to nose with the first base umpire, expressing his views in a voice loud enough for Julie to hear. The players pressed against the wire of the dugout to watch the scene. Parents on both sides yelled and ran for the fence. Chaos erupted.

Left in the stands, Julie turned to Dallas. "What did you say about it not getting any better than this?"

**VEDA BOYD JONES** writes romances "that confirm my own values." Jones lives with her husband, an architect, and three sons in the Ozarks of Missouri.

# Gentle Persuasion

*Veda Boyd Jones*

*Heartsong Presents*

For my parents, Raymond and Dorothy Boyd, with love.

Thanks to Joan Banks, Bonnie Hinman, Anita Heistand, and Elaine Jones for help in the writing of this book. And a special thanks to four baseball players, Jimmie, Landon, Morgan, and Marshall for teaching me all that I know about the game.

ISBN 1-55748-388-4

# GENTLE PERSUASION

## one

Julie Russell tapped her foot on the concrete floor of the concession stand and glanced at her watch. All customers had been waited on, and she was bored.

The American Legion ball game had gone into extra innings. Two hours had crawled by, and now with every passing minute, Julie's frustration level climbed. Cooped up in the concrete block room with two women, who, if they were to be believed, were the mothers of baseball stars, was not her idea of a great time. Even when her sixteen-year-old nephew came up to bat, she couldn't muster the enthusiasm expected of her.

Only love for her sister, Cindy, had made her volunteer to take her sister's place in the concession stand. That this could be the team's last game in the tournament and that Jimmie was the starting pitcher made the game of paramount importance to Cindy. She was sitting in the bleachers with her husband and two other sons, while Julie sweltered in the close room with a rotating fan moving the hot August air.

"I need ice and some wet paper towels," a masculine voice demanded. "We've got a jammed finger."

Julie glanced toward the man at the screen door, saw his troubled expression, and immediately turned to fill a large cup with ice. The other two concession workers stopped talking and scurried to the door to see the excitement.

"Can I help?" Julie asked, as she nudged the women out of her way and pushed the door open. She handed the towels and ice to the man.

"Yeah." He leaned toward her and said in a low voice meant for her ears only, "I'll take care of him. You take care of the mother." Julie looked behind him and saw an anxious woman huddled over a ballplayer. She was waving her hands in a distressed fashion.

"There must be a doctor in the stands," the mother shrilled as she blinked back tears.

"Here you go, Todd," the man said in a confident tone. He carefully packed the boy's finger in the ice. "This should stop the swelling so we can take a good look at your finger." With the wet paper towels, he wiped sweat off Todd's face. Then he placed the towels at the back of the young man's neck.

"Coach, do you think it's broken?" the mother asked in a high-pitched voice. "Should we call for emergency personnel?"

The player, who had remained calm through the first aid treatment, shifted uneasily from one foot to the other. The coach gave Julie a "help me out" look.

Julie breathed a silent prayer asking for guidance.

"Come get your son a cold drink," she told the woman. Julie put her hands on the mother's shoulders and turned her around, giving no opportunity for the woman to refuse. She had used that gentle form of persuasion with her students on several occasions and it never failed to work.

Julie opened the screen door and urged the mother inside the concession stand. By the time they handed cold drinks to the boy and his coach, the mother was considerably calmer. She agreed when the coach told her that Todd needed an X-ray.

"I'll check on you after the game," the man called as the boy and his mother walked toward their car.

"Thanks for helping," the coach said to Julie and strode away, leaving Julie looking after him. He was a good-looking man, dark haired, and very tall. Of course, looking up from her petite height, most people appeared very tall.

There was something else about him that she couldn't quite define. An aura of authority mixed with determination. Was it the confident way he walked, as if he knew where he was going? She watched him until he disappeared behind the dugout, then pivoted. Her sandals kicked up the dry Tribune, Missouri, summertime dust as she stepped back to the concession stand.

The last twenty minutes of the ball game flew by as Julie observed the coach. He stood beside third base, his thumbs hooked in the belt loops of his faded jeans. At times he'd go through elaborate signals, lean forward with his hands on his knees, then return to the upright position.

Julie was actually disappointed when her replacement came, followed closely by an elated Cindy.

"Great game. I really appreciate your working my shift," she said. "We won, you know. We play for the championship tomorrow."

"Great. Where's Jimmie?" Julie asked.

"Coach is talking to him and the other players. He'll be here in a minute. Be right back. I need to check the scorekeeper's schedule and see who's working tonight's game."

Cindy waved goodbye and Julie waited to offer congratulations to her nephew. Cindy and her husband,

Wade, were heavily involved in the American Legion baseball tournament. Cindy was in charge of the scorekeepers; Wade had to line up the umpires. Both had been working on the schedules for two weeks. With all the advance planning, Julie felt sure that the tournament could run on its own, but the entire Madison family virtually camped out at the ballpark during the baseball tournament.

Julie stepped toward the fence to get a look at Jimmie's team crowded around their coach. Their ecstatic faces reflected their glory in the victory.

Coach Dallas Stone finished his congratulatory talk with his habitual prayer of thanks and announced Saturday afternoon's game time. Now that the long game was over, his adrenaline had slowed down. Lazing around at a Friday night backyard barbecue appealed to him, and for once, he was glad that his sister had included him in one of her many parties. He was ready for a cold dip in the pool before returning to watch the eight o'clock game.

"What a game, Dal," his assistant said and patted him on the back. "Let's hope tomorrow's game goes like this."

"Right," Dallas called over his shoulder as he packed bats, balls, and catcher's equipment in a duffle bag.

He swung it over his shoulder with ease and walked out of the dugout with his players. Searching the crowd, he spotted the woman who had helped him with Todd's mother. Her blond hair was pulled back from her face and, although she was rather short—he guessed just over five feet—she was a knockout. Too bad she had to be some ballplayer's mother.

"Hey, Jimmie. Great game," he heard her call to his star pitcher.

"Aunt Julie," Jimmie called back. "We play for the championship tomorrow."

Maybe she wasn't a mother, after all. She sure didn't look old enough to have a sixteen-year-old son, and he hadn't noticed a ring on her finger when she was helping with Todd. He angled toward her. By the time he reached her, Jimmie was already beside her, his hand on her shoulder, obviously showing off that his height surpassed his aunt's petite frame.

"Hi," Dallas said. "Thanks again for helping me with Todd."

"Hey, Coach, was his finger broken?" Jimmie asked.

"I don't know. He's getting an X-ray." He looked into the deep blue eyes of Jimmie's aunt. "I'm Dallas Stone, Jimmie's coach."

"Julie Russell," she said and extended her slender hand. He took it in his much larger one and held it for a moment.

"Hi, Dallas." Cindy joined the group. "Have you met my little sister?" She nodded at Julie.

"Just did."

"She teaches English at the high school," Cindy informed him. "Doesn't look like an old maid schoolteacher, does she?"

"No," Dallas agreed.

"Cindy!" Julie exclaimed.

Dallas placed his free hand on Julie's shoulder and steered her off, much as she had done to Todd's mother. A few paces away, he stopped.

"I'm going to stop by the hospital and check on Todd,

then go to my sister's for a barbecue. Would you like to come with me?"

"Well," Julie began.

"I know we just met, but I'm a trustworthy guy. Just ask your sister," he said and grinned.

"All right," she answered. "I'll ask her."

His mouth dropped open. He had expected her to say an immediate yes. Most women did. No, all of them did. He hadn't been turned down yet.

Julie laughed at his expression. It was a tingling sound, a delightful sound.

"Cindy," she called to her sister. "Is Dallas trustworthy?" Dallas could feel the heat rising on his neck as others in the dwindling crowd looked toward him.

Cindy stepped over to them. "Yeah, he's trustworthy. What's up?"

Julie didn't answer her sister but looked at Dallas. "All right, I'll go with you."

"Okay," Dallas said, feeling sorry he had ever asked. "I'll follow you home so you can leave your car and pick up your swimsuit." At her raised eyebrows he continued, "It's a pool party."

"Fine," she said. "In case I lose you in traffic, I live at 402 Oak Street, three blocks from the hospital."

He nodded. "See you in a few minutes, then." He turned to talk to his assistant coach and one of his players, who had walked up behind him.

Julie said a quick goodbye to her sister in a move to avoid questions and made a beeline for her car. She had no idea why she had agreed to go out with Dallas Stone. He wasn't her type at all—a baseball coach of all things.

On the way home she chastised herself. Why had she

agreed to go with him? What was it about him that had piqued her interest? He was handsome enough. No woman over the age of two would question that. And he had an air of confidence that she admired. But a coach? What had she gotten herself into?

Her one serious romance in her twenty-four years had been in college with a basketball player. They had dated for more than a year, but their interests were too diverse for a permanent relationship. Hadn't she learned anything from that experience?

She had gone out with a coach when she had first moved back to town a year ago. Their one date had been disastrous. He had talked nonstop about sports, the only subject he knew anything about. Julie, on the other hand, knew little about sports, and cared nothing about learning more. Her opinion of athletes was equally low. Six football players were in her summer school English class trying to make up failing grades from the spring semester.

And now she had agreed to a date with another coach. She shook her head in disgust. "You're a slow learner," she said out loud.

At her little duplex, Julie packed a towel, her swimsuit, and some makeup in a tote bag. She stood looking out the picture window, waiting for Dallas. He had not pulled out of the parking lot behind her. Maybe he had changed his mind.

Dallas turned his sports car down Oak Street. He was uneasy. Why had he asked her out? Was it the way she had looked at him when he had shaken her hand? That must have been the signal his brain had automatically processed that caused him to blurt out the invitation. He had been looking forward to the party at his sister's as an opportunity to relax. He'd been keyed up all day because of the ball game. Old memories had surfaced and he wanted to erase them. Now, instead of having a good time, he had to pay attention to a date.

And she was an English teacher. He'd have to watch his grammar. Being around teachers didn't bother him. He held a teaching certificate himself, although he had never used it. English teachers, though, were another matter. He had to think about word choices, like when to use "good" or "well."

Dallas watched for Julie's address and wheeled the car into the left drive of the duplex, then saw her come out of the apartment on the right. He'd picked the wrong driveway. Did that indicate how the rest of the date would go?

Dallas hopped out of the car and opened the door for Julie. She tossed her tote bag behind her seat.

"I hope you don't mind checking on Todd."

"Not at all," she replied. "Is something wrong? You seem upset."

"No. Just a little worried about Todd. He's my best catcher."

"Oh," she said noncommittally. Dallas was fulfilling her idea of a coach—more concerned for the sport than the people involved.

They found Todd and his mother in the out-patient area, waiting for X-ray results. Julie chatted with Todd's mother, who now seemed more in control, and Dallas talked with his catcher.

Within minutes the doctor arrived and told them the finger was broken. A splint would be necessary. Todd grimaced with disappointment that he wouldn't be able to play in the final game of the tournament.

Julie was surprised at the tenderness Dallas displayed. He stayed with Todd while the finger was being set and asked him to be the team scorekeeper and general assistant for the last game.

"Wear your uniform like the other players," he told Todd.

When the doctor had finished, Julie and Dallas walked Todd and his mother to their car, then climbed into Dallas's car.

"You were very good with him," Julie said. "As if you understood his disappointment."

"I do understand. I've been there myself."

"Oh? How?"

He hesitated, as if he didn't want to talk about it, but suddenly the words came tumbling out. When he had first come to town to open up his sporting goods store, everyone had asked him about his short career as a major league baseball player. He had had four great years in college on a baseball scholarship and one year in the minors. Then his big break had come. He had been moved up to the majors in midseason and had played for four years. As a starting pitcher, he had amassed an amazing strike-out record. He'd even pitched two no-hitters. The skiing accident that had broken his back in two places had ended his dream.

"So you do know the disappointment," Julie said. "Does it still hurt?"

"My back has healed fine, but it can't take the strain of pitching."

"I meant the pain of leaving baseball."

"Yeah, it still hurts."

"You were blessed. You had your dream for a little while. A lot of people aren't that fortunate," Julie told him.

He parked the car at the curb in front of a one-story brick house and sat looking at her for a long moment.

"You're right," he finally said, nodding in agreement. "When it first happened, I kept asking, 'Why me, God?' I still don't know why, but I've come to accept it."

"Maybe God has another purpose for you," Julie said.

"Maybe," he answered. "Let's go."

Instead of knocking on the front door, Dallas led Julie to the backyard gate. Laughter, the smell of barbecued ribs, and the sounds of splashing water told them the party was in full swing.

Julie met too many people to remember, but concentrated on Dallas's sister Marti and her husband, Hal.

"Come in here to change," Marti instructed and led Julie into the house and to a bedroom.

As soon as she had donned her suit, Julie returned to the pool to find Dallas already in the water. She dove in and swam toward him. After a spirited game of team water volleyball with the two playing on opposing sides, they climbed out, arguing about a call.

By the time they had dried off, the sun had sunk below the horizon and the meat was ready. They loaded paper plates with ribs, potato salad, and baked beans. Julie sat in a lawn chair; Dallas sat beside her on the tiled deck.

"How did you meet Dallas?" Marti inquired as she sat down in the chair next to Julie.

"At a baseball game," Julie answered between bites.

"Oh. A sports enthusiast," Marti said. From the way

she glanced at Dallas, Julie thought Marti really meant, "Oh. A baseball groupie."

"Actually, I don't care for sports," Julie said, in self-defense. "I attended the game only because my nephew was playing."

"Don't like sports?" Marti's husband asked. Dallas remained quiet, but watched Julie carefully.

"I think all the money spent on sports in schools could be better spent on books and other educational needs."

"Really?" Dallas said with a frown. "A lot of people feel that way, but sports have their place, too."

"Competition on a playing field doesn't lead to feelings of camaraderie. How can you maintain good feelings toward someone who is trying to make you lose? For example, a little while ago in the water, we were on opposite teams. Did you feel friendship and kindness toward me, or did you want to win, no matter what?"

"What I felt was not friendship and kindness, but something a bit stronger," he flirted with her.

The others laughed, but Julie thought that he was fitting her stereotype of a coach. *Don't be judgmental,* she told herself. *Give him the benefit of the doubt.* His gentle treatment of Todd, his explanation of his own disappointment because of an injury had made her think that the coach in him was merely a facade. He had a business, although related to athletics, which required a common sense approach. Those qualities, along with the magnetic pull that she felt toward Dallas, had given her hope that he was an intelligent, caring, Christian individual. She didn't want that illusion destroyed.

"Thanks for inviting us," Dallas said to his brother-in-law. "We need to get back to the ballpark.

Tomorrow we play the winner of tonight's game."

"A little scouting, huh?" Hal asked.

"Exactly. Shall we go, Julie?"

After they had both changed out of their swimsuits, Dallas drove them back to the baseball field.

"Why don't you like sports?" he asked as he sat down beside her on the bleachers.

"I believe they're overemphasized."

"Yes, you said that. What other reason?"

"Isn't one enough?"

"I don't think so."

"Okay," she said, and was amazed that she was going to tell him. "I'm from an athletic family. My three brothers played every sport you can imagine. Cindy was an outstanding softball player. But I'm not oriented that way. Sports don't interest me. I'd rather spend my time with a book than watching a sports event. I'm good at research, analyzing things, academic subjects. But to my family, that's nothing." She smoothed back her hair with an agitated gesture.

"I was valedictorian of my class," she continued, shifting on the wooden bleacher, "but that was not nearly as important to my family as my brother making the all-conference football team. In college when I was inducted into Phi Theta Kappa, the academic honorary society, they didn't even come."

Dallas nodded. "And that hurt," he stated.

"Yes. I've often asked God if He plunked me down in the wrong family. Not that I don't love them," she quickly explained. "They're all hard-working, Christian people. I just don't seem to fit in."

"Sounds like a little compromise is needed on both

sides. Sports may be too important to your family, but athletics have a place, too."

"Oh?" she said, feeling that she had compromised with sports all her life. She couldn't believe she was back at the ballpark watching a game when she wasn't related to a single player. If she hadn't wanted to get to know Dallas better, she would have asked him to take her directly home from the party. As it was, she'd probably alienated him with her opinion of sports. And she shouldn't have confided in him about her family. People were supposed to support their families, no matter what.

"Take baseball," he said and climbed on his own soapbox. "You're competing against nine other players, but at the same time you're building fellowship and cooperation between the nine players on your team. They depend on you to do your part and you depend on them to do their jobs. That's the way it is in the work force, which is also part of life."

"I see." Julie digested his statements and, although not totally agreeing, had to acknowledge that he might have some valid points. "You're very persuasive. I'll give it some thought."

"Good," Dallas said and reached for her hand. "Now, will you come see my team play tomorrow?"

"I'll be there," Julie answered and immediately wondered why she had so readily agreed.

At that moment, Julie saw her sister walk in front of the bleachers, scanning the crowd. When she spotted Julie sitting with Dallas, Cindy's mouth dropped open.

"Would you like a Coke?" Dallas asked as Cindy climbed the bleacher stairs toward them.

"That sounds good," Julie answered.

"Be right back."

Julie watched him stop a moment on the steps and say something to Cindy.

"What are you doing here?" Cindy asked as she sat down beside Julie.

"Watching a ball game."

"Get real, Julie. Listen, Dallas isn't your type."

"Oh? He seems nice enough." Her brow creased in concern. "You mean he's not a Christian?"

"Julie." Cindy waved her hands in exasperation, as if she wasn't getting through to her sister. "He goes to our church," she said as if explaining something to a child.

"He does? I've never seen him there."

"He goes to late service. But that's not what I mean. He's an athlete—a professional one, at that. He's a great guy, but he's not for you."

"You're probably right, Cindy, but we're just on a date. We're not getting married."

Cindy studied her sister and Julie looked away, unwilling to discuss Dallas any further. She didn't know what she felt toward Dallas, but she didn't want Cindy's advice. Her gaze fell on Dallas, who was climbing the stairs, balancing two drinks and a bag of popcorn.

"You're in Dallas's seat," Julie told her sister.

"I just don't want you to get hurt," Cindy said softly and stood up. She moved into the aisle as Dallas claimed his seat beside Julie.

# two

Although Julie sat on the shaded part of the bleachers, she could feel perspiration bead on her forehead and knew the temperature had to be close to one hundred. She fanned herself with her hand.

"Pretty hot out here," she said. "Would you like a Coke, Cindy? I need something to cool me off. What inning is it?"

"Bottom of the second," Cindy answered.

Julie should have known that. She had watched Dallas as he stood out by third base when his team batted. Now he was on the far side of the dugout, out of her sight.

"Anyone else want anything?" Julie asked and took drink orders from her brother-in-law and nephew. She climbed down from the stands and sauntered to the concession stand. It made her feel cooler just knowing she didn't have to be cooped up in the concrete building handing out refreshments.

"Our guys are ahead by one," the woman in line ahead of her said to her companion.

"Let's hope they can stretch that lead. All that practice has paid off. I'll admit I complained when Mel called practice every night for the last three weeks, but he knows what he's doing," the other woman said.

"Your son practiced ball every night?" Julie asked, astonishment in her voice.

"Except when we had games," the woman answered. "Takes a lot of practice to work as a team," she added defensively. She exchanged a look with the other

19

woman, then turned away from Julie, discouraging any
further conversation.

Julie moved up in line, got four drinks, and balanced
them precariously as she walked back to the stands.

"Cindy, is that Mel Cooney out there coaching the
other team?" Julie asked once she was settled back down
on the hard bleacher.

"You know him?"

"He teaches business at the high school. I didn't
recognize him in a ball cap. I knew he lived in Gentry
and drove up here to teach, but I didn't know he coached
the Gentry team. I should have noticed him last night."
But last night she had been too aware of Dallas beside
her to concentrate on the game.

"I'm surprised to see you again today," Cindy said.
Her attention shifted from the ball field to Julie. "How
did Dallas get you back here?"

"He asked me to come," Julie said simply and quickly
shifted the subject. "Look, Dallas is going to take out the
pitcher."

"That's Brad Williams. He's usually pretty good, but
he's wild today. Too bad Jimmie pitched yesterday. He
can't pitch again so soon. Might hurt his arm."

"Brad Williams? I should have recognized him. He's
in my class this summer." Julie peered at the players and
recognized a few more that she had taught or had seen in
school. "Those caps block their faces," she said.

Julie watched Dallas stride out to the pitcher's mound.
He placed his hand on Brad's shoulder and talked to
him, then walked back to the dugout.

"Guess he's going to give him a chance to settle
down," Wade commented. "We have only three good

pitchers," he explained to his sister-in-law.

The game dragged on and on.

"Last inning," Cindy finally announced. "Our last chance to catch up."

Julie glanced at the scoreboard. Five to seven.

Even with a valiant effort by Dallas's team, the game ended with Mel Cooney's team winning.

"Too bad," Julie said to her sister, but she was relieved the game was over.

"Yeah," Cindy said, disappointment etched on her face. The fourth inning killed us. You can't allow that many hits." She paced back and forth in front of the stands.

In the dugout, Dallas studied the long faces of his players.

"We played a good game, even though we were out-scored. And I'm proud of each of you. We've had a good season. We're out here to learn to be better ball-players, be team players, and to have a good time. Let's thank God that we've been given that opportunity."

After the boys bowed their heads for a moment in silent prayer, Dallas said, "Amen. Now to celebrate our successful season, I'm buying pizza for the whole team. Six-thirty at my house. Hope you all can come." He dismissed the team and started packing the duffle bag with bats and the catcher's equipment.

"Hey, coach, I've got a date. Can she come?" one player asked.

"If you already have a date, bring her. If not, just come on over," he announced to his players.

As the boys moved slowly out of the dugout, Dallas searched the stands for Julie. He had seen her earlier, but he couldn't find her now. People were standing on the bleachers and climbing down, so he didn't have a clear view.

"Good game, Dallas."

He turned to find Julie standing at the entrance to the dugout and wondered how long she'd been there.

"Thanks. They played a good game," he agreed. "So we're having a pizza party at my house. No sense in ending the season on a down note."

Julie glanced back over her shoulder where a few of the boys were still close to the dugout talking in low tones.

"Think that will do it?" she asked.

"It's hard losing the championship this close. They're down now, but by the time they get to my house, they'll have put it in perspective and be ready to party. Will you come, too?" he asked. He really wanted her there.

"Sure," Julie answered and flashed a thousand-watt smile. "What time?"

"Around six. You can help me get ready for the guys." He glanced at his watch. "Well, why don't you come now? It's already four."

"I'll follow you," Julie volunteered.

It was nearly four-thirty before they managed to leave the ballpark. People loitered, not wanting to call an end to the baseball season. Cindy and Wade were surrounded by people replaying the game. Dallas was cornered by more of the same types.

Julie hovered at the edge of the crowd, waiting. She didn't belong to this group, but that didn't bother her. She had little in common with these people and wouldn't see many of them until next year's tournament, if she was conned into working the concession stand again.

"Ready?" Dallas said as he walked up beside her. "I'll follow you home, then you can ride with me."

"That's not necessary," Julie said. "I can follow you, then you won't have to drive me home later." That would also allow her to leave whenever she was ready, instead of when the last ballplayer decided the party was over.

Dallas drove slowly allowing Julie plenty of time to follow his signals. He turned onto Winfield Avenue in the older part of town. Large maple trees lined both sides of the street. He drove three blocks, then pulled into the drive of a contemporary-style house.

The garage door opened, and he pulled forward. Julie parked behind him in the drive. Before she could unbuckle her seat belt, Dallas was beside her, opening her door.

"Come on in," he said, as he led her through the garage and into the utility room. "I'll put you to work."

"I knew there was a reason you wanted me here. I must warn you, I love pizza. Probably could eat my weight in it. So I shall extract my reward for any elbow grease expended."

He laughed and walked her through the kitchen and into the high-beamed living room. It was a lived-in room with a stone fireplace that reached twelve feet high and bookcases that covered one entire wall. Overstuffed chairs and a couch with throw pillows added to the comfortable feeling. The room was immaculate.

"Why do you need help? I expected a typical bachelor pad with dirty plates and glasses on the coffee table and clothes on the floor."

"I'm a neat guy," Dallas said and grinned. "I also have a cleaning lady who came this morning."

"What can I do?" Julie asked.

"We need to ice down some pop. The cans are cold, but I'd like to have them in a cooler. We'll have the party on the back porch."

The back porch was a huge, screened-in room with wrought iron table and chairs in the center and other chairs and small tables scattered around the edges.

"This is a great place for a party," Julie said as she carried a twelve-pack of soft drinks out to Dallas. He placed them in a cooler and covered that layer with ice. Julie returned to the refrigerator to get more cans.

Besides pop, there was little else in the refrigerator. Jars of mayonnaise, mustard, and a squeeze bottle of ketchup had her guessing that he ate sandwiches quite a bit. A carton of eggs, bacon, some link sausages, three cans of refrigerated biscuits, and a jar of jelly told her that he liked breakfast.

She carried another case out to the screened-in porch. This was her second time to be with Dallas. Both times had involved baseball and a party. She felt that there was more to him than that, and she wanted to see him in a different environment.

"What's next?" she asked as Dallas finished packing the last of the ice in the cooler. "Paper plates?"

"I forgot about those. Guess I figured they'd hold the pizza in their hands. We'll have to run to the store. Anything else we might need?"

"Napkins?"

"I have those."

"I'll go get plates if you have something else you need to do," Julie offered.

"No. We have plenty of time," he said and ushered her toward the door. "Would you move your car?"

"Oh, I'll drive," Julie offered.

At the grocery store, Dallas selected plain white plates. Julie held up some pretty ones decorated with daisies.

"Never," he said. "My players are not chauvinists," he said quickly, "but they are males."

Dallas was wrong about them having plenty of time. They had barely returned to his house, set the table with a stack of plates and napkins, and decided how many pizzas they'd need to feed thirteen hungry high school boys, when the doorbell rang.

"Are we too early, Coach?" one of the boys asked as he and another boy faced Dallas.

Dallas glanced at his watch. It was only five-thirty. He knew he had told them an hour later.

"We didn't have nothing else to do," the boy said.

"Anything else to do," Dallas corrected him. After all, there was an English teacher in the house. "Come on in," he said and motioned for them to follow.

This was not what he had planned. He had wanted time to talk to Julie, get to know her, but all they had done was get things organized. They had just sat down with a cold drink when the boys appeared.

He introduced them to Julie. "Help yourself to some pop. You can play Frisbee if you'd like." He pointed to the round disk on a side table. One of the boys picked it up and whirled it at the other one. "Out in the yard," Dallas added.

"Yeah, Coach." The two boys took their drinks and slammed the screen door as they ran outside.

"Sorry. I told them six-thirty."

"When should we order the pizza?"

"Oh, not yet. There won't be any more coming for a while." The end of his statement was punctuated by the ringing of the doorbell.

Dallas returned from the door with three more players.

"Hello, Cleve," Julie said.

"Hi, Miss Russell. Jimmie here?" he asked, obviously wondering about her presence.

"Miss Russell's my date tonight," Dallas said smoothly and introduced the other two boys.

"Cleve was in my junior English class last year," Julie explained as soon as they were alone. "Several of your players were students of mine. One of your pitchers, Brad Williams, is in my summer school class."

"You'll have a lot more of them come September," Dallas said. "We have a young team. If we'd had more eighteen-year-olds, we might have won today. Actually, we've had a great season for as young a team as we have. We'll be hard to beat next year."

"Maybe your prayers will be answered."

"What do you mean?" he asked.

"I heard your speech to the boys after the game. You all thanked God for a good season. Did you pray before the game, too? Did you ask to win?"

"No. Well, yes, we said a prayer, but we only asked that each player be allowed to play his best."

"I've often wondered if both teams prayed to win."

"I don't know about the other team, but I've always felt that asking Him to choose wouldn't be fair."

"Interesting," Julie mused and was about to expand on his remark when the doorbell rang again.

"I think we'd better order that pizza," Dallas said on his way into the house.

This time Dallas ushered in a player and his date, who took chairs on the porch instead of joining the boys in the yard with the Frisbee. Julie visited with them while Dallas called for pizza delivery.

Conversation on the porch was stilted. Julie knew that many students were stunned when they saw teachers out of the classroom. Once she had seen a student at the grocery store, and he had actually said, "You come to the grocery store?" as if she didn't eat like a normal person. This couple had the same look on their faces as they stared at a teacher sitting on the coach's porch.

When the doorbell rang again, Julie excused herself and answered the door since Dallas was still on the phone.

"Jimmie, come on in," she said, glad it was her nephew so she wouldn't feel so uncomfortable.

"What are you doing here, Aunt Julie?" he asked at once. "Oh, you're dating Coach," he answered his own question.

"Well, I'm helping him with this party," she answered. She was about to shut the door to keep the hot air outside when another car pulled up and unloaded two couples. Then another car arrived and another.

By six o'clock, twelve players and five girlfriends were on the back porch or in the yard.

"We're missing Brad," Dallas said. "Anybody know if he's coming?"

No one knew. Julie doubted that he'd show up. From

her limited knowledge of him, she thought he was antisocial. In class, he rarely spoke and only when she forced him to answer a question.

Dallas mixed easily with his ballplayers. Julie was an outsider, just as she had been at the baseball park. The high schoolers were high-spirited and full of energy even on such a hot August evening, but they tiptoed around her.

"You like pizza, Miss Russell?" one of the players asked as she reached for her third piece. Again there was that astonishment that a teacher could like something that a student liked.

"Pepperoni's my favorite," she said and smiled.

Talk naturally turned to baseball and the afternoon's game.

"The thing is," one player said, "those guys played together all spring on Gentry's high school team. They were a cinch to win the tournament."

Jimmie turned to his aunt, but announced to the group in general, "What we need is a high school team. Can we have one?" he asked her as if she were a school board member and could decide that issue.

"The high school has a large number of sports programs already. We're there to teach academics. We're not a training ground for athletics." She knew she sounded stuffy, but she was being truthful.

"We have football and basketball," Cleve spoke up. "Why can't we have baseball?"

The entire group stared at Julie. She glanced at Dallas. His face was a question mark, too.

## three

Dallas looked up from his desk as his partner, Alex McBain, came into his office.

"Think it's time for the fifty percent sign to go up?" Alex asked.

Dallas knew his partner was referring to the baseball shirts that featured professional athletes. They marked down other baseball equipment, such as bats, gloves, pants, and shoes, for only one week, and they had already run that sale. Although they had unloaded quite a bit of merchandise, what was left was being shifted to the large back room. It would sell in the spring.

"All right by me," Dallas answered. He rarely questioned Alex's judgement.

Dallas had been in the retail sporting goods business for six months. Alex had worked in stores like theirs for almost two decades. Dallas was the money behind the store; Alex was the know-how. Many times Dallas felt he was fooling himself if he thought he really earned his keep. He was good with figures and kept a close eye on receipts and expenditures, but Alex could guess the profit without even looking at the books.

"Saw in the paper that you lost to Gentry," Alex said, referring to Saturday's game.

"Yeah. Tough game. Most of their players were on the high school team, so they had a lot of practice together before the Legion season started."

"You know, we should have a high school team," Alex said.

"I've been thinking the same thing," Dallas said. "My players don't see why we can't. Gentry's a smaller town than Tribune and they have a team."

"They got that team by private enterprise," Alex said. "Be back," he said when the bell jingled over the front door signaling a customer had entered.

"Morning, Howard." Alex's greeting to the business-man who owned the computer store next door in the shopping center drifted back to Dallas. He glanced at his watch. Ten–thirty on the nose. Howard was never late for a coffee break.

Curiosity forced Dallas to push back his chair.

"Alex," he called from the office doorway. He walked toward the men as he spoke. "Before you leave, tell me about Gentry's high school team."

"A committee raised the money to finance it for the first couple years. After that, the school district took over."

Howard jumped right into the conversation. "You thinking of getting a high school team in Tribune?"

"Well," Dallas hedged. He hadn't thought far enough ahead to answer that question. "Just wondering why we didn't have one."

"You could do it," Howard said. "Big pitcher like you start a campaign, the whole town would go for it."

"I'll think about it," Dallas said.

A customer walked in jingling the bell above the door. Alex glanced at Dallas.

"Go on. I'll take care of this," Dallas said.

He waited on the customer, then settled down on the stool behind the cash register. Monday mornings were usually slow, so they didn't have extra help until afternoon. In the quiet of the brightly lit store, his thoughts turned to the high school team.

Julie had been dead set against another sport at the high school. That fit with what she had said Friday night at the Gentry game about sports being overemphasized. Her family had certainly turned her against sports.

He had placed her in an awkward position at his pizza party. He hadn't considered her having some of his players in class. They felt as ill at ease around an English teacher as he usually did. Julie had held her own, but they had excluded her from the group in subtle ways.

There was something about her that excited him. He had to admit that he didn't usually go for the school-teacher type, but he liked the intelligent look in her eyes that warred with an elusive sense of fun that he guessed she didn't allow to surface very often. Instinctively he knew that getting to know her would be an uphill battle because of her dislike for athletics, which he represented.

"How do I impress her?" he said aloud to the empty store. Although the store was devoid of customers, he felt God's presence and talked to Him. "What do I do?"

He laughed at himself. He usually didn't have to worry about impressing women. This was a whole new ball game for him.

He decided to call Julie after school and ask her to dinner. A nonbaseball date. Then maybe she could see him as an individual, not as a sports figure.

The bell above the door announced the return of Alex and Howard from the coffee shop. They were full of plans for the "Baseball for Tribune High School Committee."

"We're drafting you as chairman," Howard said. "Your name will bring lots of support."

Julie called on a student and asked him to read Robert Frost's "The Road Not Taken." She had another student read "Stopping By Woods on a Snowy Evening."

Frost was her favorite poet. She liked his introspection and hoped to teach the students to look inward for understanding. By the last week of summer school, her students were unsettled and ready for the three week break before the regular school year began. Poetry was an easy way to end the course. She assigned no homework. Instead they discussed the poetry in class. On the last day, the students would write an in-class paper comparing poets' styles.

Julie called on Brad Williams, who seemed very inattentive, and had him explain which road the poet had taken. He stuttered around. Another student explained the poem and then Julie asked Brad his opinion again.

"Which road in life will you choose?" she asked him.

He merely shrugged.

Teaching summer school was hard. There were those in her class who excelled and wanted to gain extra credits in the summer, and there were those who had already failed the class once and were making it up. There was no middle ground. Teaching to both ends of the spectrum was nearly impossible, but Julie did her best by involving the students in discussions instead of lecturing to them.

It was a mistake to label all the athletes as being in the lower part of the class. Two of them were excellent students. But as a whole, she would have to agree there was reason for the stereotype of "dumb jock." They might not be so dumb, but they were so single-minded that subjects other than sports didn't matter.

Athletes brought to mind the events of Saturday night. She had left before the party was over. Everyone had turned to her with the issue of getting a baseball team for the high school. Not only did she not have any authority to give them an answer, she didn't want another sport added to the curriculum.

The bell rang. "Tomorrow we'll read a few of Carl Sandburg's poems. See you then," she said.

The students sauntered out. Some would head for the swimming pool at the park. Others had afternoon jobs. None of them, Julie was sure, would spend the afternoon reading "Chicago" in preparation for the next day.

Back in her duplex, Julie changed into shorts and fixed a big glass of iced tea and half a ham sandwich. She carried her lunch and her literature book out onto the patio in back and prepared for the next class. Within minutes she was deep into the harsh images of Sandburg's city. She had been to Chicago only once, but the poem fit the rawness of the city and the pride of its people. Daydreams of her visit filled her mind—the sailboats on Lake Michigan, the museums and restaurants, the huge homes on the Gold Coast.

A faint ringing brought her back to Tribune, Missouri, on a humid August afternoon. Julie ran inside and answered the telephone on the sixth ring.

She recognized Dallas's voice immediately, and her heart started beating double time.

"What time did the party break up?" she asked.

"Not long after you left. As soon as all the pizza and

pop were gone," he said and laughed. Julie laughed, too.

"I was hoping you'd go out to dinner with me tonight," Dallas said. "We didn't get much of a chance to talk Saturday night. I had no idea those guys would show up that early."

"One never knows what teenagers will do," Julie said.

"I saw you leave church yesterday."

"I didn't see you," Julie said.

"Actually, I was driving in the parking lot when you were leaving. So, what about tonight?"

"I'd love to go."

"Great. I'll pick you up at seven," Dallas said.

After his phone call, Julie couldn't settle down to poetry again. *Why does he make me feel so out of control?* she wondered. She didn't want to be with him, yet she could hardly wait until he arrived. In frustration, she swung into a cleaning frenzy and had her little duplex shining within two hours. As a reward, she poured a big glass of cola and relaxed in the bathtub with a magazine.

The debate of what to wear on her date lasted through four outfits. Shorts might be too casual, a silk dress too formal. Finally she chose a yellow striped sun dress and sandals.

It was the right choice. Dallas arrived precisely at seven wearing khaki chinos and a navy golf shirt.

"Do you like Chinese food?" he asked as he opened the passenger door for her.

"Sounds great," she said. "I haven't been to The Fortune Cookie in some time."

Dallas drove them to the only Chinese restaurant in town.

"This place isn't bad," he said. "I think the sweet-and-sour pork is the best thing on the menu."

"Do you eat here often?"

"I love Chinese food. I know the best Chinese restaurant in every city where we played ball. From New York to San Francisco, I've eaten moo goo gai pan."

"This is really a different life for you, isn't it? Small town, running a sporting goods store, no longer a jet setter."

"I'm happy here. I'll admit I miss baseball. That's why I coached the Legion team. Keeps me in the game."

"Why'd you come to Tribune?"

"My sister had married and settled here. I had no special place to go, and I didn't want to live in Chicago anymore since I couldn't play. I got the idea of a sporting goods shop, so I prayed about it. Things started falling into place. The market would allow a sporting goods store here, so I decided on Tribune. I found Alex, my partner, and a shop to rent. I bought a house I fell in love with and the rest is history. I've been here for six months now. Tea?" he asked. Julie nodded and he poured tea into two small, handleless cups.

"I figured I'd give the store two years to break even and five years to turn a good profit. If it didn't, I'd try something else."

"What would something else be?" Julie asked and took a sip of her hot tea.

"I'm not sure. I have a degree in business and a teaching certificate. My dad emphasized the importance of getting an education along with playing college ball. His favorite saying was 'God helps those who help themselves.' He believed a sports career was for a short period of time, and I would have to be able to support myself after baseball. He was sure right," Dallas added with a sigh.

"You didn't care for Chicago?" Julie asked, remembering the poem she had read just a few hours before.

"I liked it. But everywhere I looked were reminders that I couldn't play ball anymore. My friends were ball-players, and during the season they'd be gone most of the time. I'm from a small Kentucky town. I remember a slower pace of life and I'm all for that. What about you? Why Tribune?"

"I'm home. I was born here. I went away to college and worked one year in Kansas City before a job opened up here. I liked the city, but like you, I felt a pull toward a simpler life." She laughed. "I don't know that life is simpler in a small town, though. There are still the same twenty-four-hour days, and they fill up fast."

"Your family lives here? I know your sister does."

"My parents live on a farm west of Tribune. My two older brothers live here in town, and I have a younger brother who goes to college in Joplin."

"Do you see a lot of them?" he asked. The waiter arrived with their food, and Julie waited until the dishes had been arranged on the table to answer.

"During the week we talk on the phone. Most Sundays after church we have a big family dinner at the farm. Would you like some of this pepper steak?"

"Sure. Try this," Dallas said and handed her the sweet-and-sour dish.

"What do your brothers do for a living?" he then asked.

"John works for the electric company and Merle

works for the water company. We have a family joke about the utilities on the Monopoly board. They're both in management—actually have equivalent jobs. I'm not sure what Tom will do when he gets out of college. He's getting a business degree, too.

"You said you have a teaching certificate," Julie added. "Have you ever thought of teaching?" She was enjoying dinner. Finding out all the first-date things was interesting. She liked Dallas. And she was finally relaxing around him. Her heartbeat had returned to normal.

"No. I got certified because it was important to my dad. He was a teacher. I would have majored in baseball, but he said to find compatible areas. Business would force me to be aware of finances, he reasoned, and a teaching certificate would come in handy if I ever wanted to coach."

"Your dad sounds like a wise man."

"He was. He died of a heart attack three years ago. My mom still lives in Kentucky. Another sister lives there, too. I thought of starting my sporting goods store there, but the town already had one. More rice?"

"No, thanks. This is good."

"Perhaps we can fly to Joplin sometime. It has several Chinese places."

"Fly to Joplin?"

"I need the hours." At her puzzled expression, Dallas explained. "I'm a pilot. I need to log hours to keep my license."

"Did you become a pilot so you could fly to ball games?"

"No. We flew commercially as a team. I've been a pilot for years. I worked at the airport during high school in exchange for flying lessons." He laid his fork down and gave her his full attention.

"Do you know the poem 'High Flight'? 'Oh, I have slipped the surly bonds of earth and danced the skies on laughter-silvered wings.' "

Dallas quoted the rest of the poem and Julie joined him in the last line: "And I touched the face of God."

Dallas reached for her hand. "That's what it's like. Do you like to fly?"

"I've never flown in a small plane."

"We'll have to fix that," he said and smiled.

Julie smiled back at Dallas. It would be nice to go out with him again. Certainly it had been a pleasant evening. Although they had touched on baseball because it was important in his life, they had not dwelled on it. He wasn't self-centered, and he seemed genuinely interested in her background.

He was the most well-balanced athlete she'd ever met. Nothing like the high school coach she had gone out with that one time. Nothing like her brothers who ate, drank, and slept sports. And what a relief it was to find a Christian man who had other interests than athletics. A man who could quote poetry.

She wanted to ask Dallas's opinion on the special city election coming up and find out if he tended to be conservative or liberal. She wanted to know what he did in his spare time. Did he have any hobbies other than flying? What was his favorite book?

She was about to ask when a man approached their table. He looked at Julie, then zeroed in on Dallas.

"Dal, I think it's wonderful that you're going to head the committee," he said and slapped him on the back.

"Hello, Lon. I'll bet you've talked to Howard."

"He called me this afternoon. I don't know why we didn't think of this before. It'll be great. I've got a friend in Gentry, and I'm going to find out how they did it. Who they hit up for big money, that sort of thing."

"Julie, I'd like you to meet Lon Feldman. Lon, Julie Russell."

"Nice to meet you," Julie murmured.

"Hi," he said and looked her over in a way Julie didn't like. "Isn't it great? If anybody can do it, Dal can."

"Do what?" Julie asked, forcing a smile at the man.

"Get Tribune a high school baseball team."

## *four*

"A baseball team for the high school?" Julie echoed.

"It'll be great. With Dal as the chairman, the committee will raise the money in no time."

Dallas glanced at Julie and back at Lon. "We shouldn't get overly optimistic," he said. "We'll just see how it goes Thursday night."

"I'm spreading the word to anybody interested," Lon said. "I'll bet we get the money within a month."

"We'll see," Dallas said again. "Good to see you, Lon." Dallas raised his eyebrows at Lon to give him the message to beat it.

Lon grinned at him and winked at Julie. "I'll see you later, Dal. Bye, Julie."

"What committee?" Julie asked, sitting up straighter in her chair.

Dallas explained about Gentry's ball team and how they had raised the money to finance the team for the first few years.

"We're aiming for three years operating expenses," he said. "But the whole thing may come to nothing. It's just an idea. More tea?"

"Yes, please." Obviously Dallas wanted to change the subject, and Julie agreed with that tactic. She smiled and picked up her fork.

They finished the meal without any other interruptions.

"How about a walk around the square?" Dallas suggested as they exited the restaurant.

"Good idea," Julie agreed and fell in step with him.

Tribune had grown around the county court house that sat in the middle of a square block. Businesses and offices lined the four streets that surrounded the square. Although there were several shopping centers on the edge of town, Tribune's business center still remained downtown. Had there been a vacancy, Dallas would have rented space on the square for his sporting goods store.

Other couples and groups walked the square or sat on the park benches around the court house. Traffic was heavy because the driving route for the teenage crowd started at the square, went out McCord Street to McDonald's, circled it, and doubled back to the square again. It was the place to see and be seen.

Dallas reached down and took Julie's hand as they crossed the street and started up another side. "Don't want you to get lost," he told her and grinned.

"Hey, Julie." At the sound Julie turned toward the street and waved as she saw her brother John go by.

"I think you're about to meet my brother," she said. She watched John's car pass the turnoff that led to his part of town. After circling the square, he pulled in by the curb a few yards ahead of them. He got out of his car and leaned on the bumper, waiting to intercept them.

"Evening, Julie," he said but looked at Dallas.

"Hi, John. I'd like you to meet Dallas Stone. Dallas, my brother John Russell."

"I've been wanting to meet you ever since you came to town. I've been in your store, but I always missed you. What a ballplayer!" John said and enthusiastically pumped Dallas's hand. "I hear you're heading up the baseball committee. About time we had a high school team."

"We just talked about it this morning," Dallas said. "How did you hear about it so fast?"

"Howard called the electric company to reserve our meeting room for Thursday night. It's a good place to start. We can seat about a hundred. You coming, Julie?"

Julie gave him a piercing look. "Get real, John."

John laughed. "I didn't think so. She's not one for sports," he told Dallas.

"I picked up on that. How do we change her mind?" Dallas asked.

"Doubt we can. She's the only non-sports minded one in the family. Can't figure it out."

"Were you headed someplace special?" Julie asked.

"Oops," John said as he glanced at his watch. "I've got to pick up Teresa from a friend's house. I'll see you Thursday night, Dallas."

"Teresa's my niece," Julie explained as they continued their walk. "John has three daughters, Teresa, Tamera, and Tracy. Three Ts. It's very confusing. I mix up their names all the time."

"Hey, Julie." Julie again looked toward the street and waved.

"I don't believe this," she said. "It must be the Russells' night out. You're about to meet my parents."

They walked to the parking spot where Julie's father had maneuvered his car.

"Hi, Mom, Dad. I'd like you to meet Dallas Stone. Dallas, my parents, Charles and Evelyn Russell." After the exchange of pleasantries, Julie asked where the older Russells were headed.

"We drove into town to get ice cream," Charles said. "Your mother just had to have a chocolate dipped cone. Why don't you join us?"

"Well," Julie hedged.

"A fine idea," Dallas said. "We had only a fortune cookie for dessert."

Julie and Dallas climbed into the back seat and soon the foursome was sitting at a picnic table outside the Dairy Queen eating ice cream. Charles and Dallas kept up a running conversation that centered on Charles's questions about baseball and Dallas's pro career.

"He seems nice," Evelyn said in a quiet voice to Julie.

"Yes," Julie said.

"An athlete, dear?" Evelyn said with a twinkle in her eye. "God moves in mysterious ways."

"I know," Julie said. This time His moves were so mysterious, she hadn't figured them out. One moment she thought Dallas was Mr. Wonderful and the next moment she found out he was as obsessed by sports as her family. "There's a committee forming to get a high school baseball team, and Dallas is the chairman."

"What's that about a high school team?" Charles asked.

Dallas explained about the committee.

"Do you think Jimmie might get to play on the team?"

"Good possibility," Dallas said. "He's a hustler. Will he be a junior?"

"Yeah. He'd have two years to play if you get that team going this year. Is that the plan?"

"I hope so," Dallas said. "The people I've spoken with are enthusiastic. If we're going to make a go of it, we've got to aim for this spring. John's coming to the meeting

Thursday night."

"I'll be there, too," Charles said. "I know you can count on Wade and Cindy. The Russells are a baseball family." He glanced at Julie. "Except for one."

Julie gave a resigned smile.

"I know," Dallas said. He glanced at Julie and grinned.

"Too bad about the game Saturday," Charles said. "I wonder how far the Gentry team will get in the state tournament."

"It's in Springfield this year," Dallas said. "I thought I'd go watch a couple of games Saturday. Gentry plays a Legion team from Columbia. Ought to be a good game."

"Julie, are you coming for Sunday dinner? Tom will be home," Charles said. "You ought to bring this fellow along."

"I don't know if he's ready to meet the whole clan," Julie answered, trying to get Dallas off the hook. He'd been gracious enough to join her parents for ice cream. She wasn't going to serve him a massive dose of family.

"Sounds like fun," Dallas said.

"That's settled then," said Charles.

"Good," Julie said. "If you're all through, I need to be getting back. Only four more days of summer school, but I have to be prepared."

"What are you studying?" Evelyn asked as they piled back into the car and headed downtown.

"Poetry. Frost and Sandburg."

"Frost is one of my favorites," Dallas said and quoted the end of "Stopping By Woods on a Snowy Evening."

Julie was impressed. "He's my favorite, too," she said. After they had left her parents, Dallas drove Julie home.

"I was hoping you'd go with me to Springfield Saturday," Dallas said, standing under the glare of the front porch light. "We could make a day of it, starting with breakfast. What do you say?"

"Go with you to the baseball tournament?" She couldn't believe he was asking her to yet another sporting event. She should refuse.

"Yes. Take in a couple of games and any other sites you'd like to see in Springfield. Be an easy day—a celebration of school's being out."

"All right," she said against her better judgment.

"Great," Dallas said. "I'll pick you up around seven."

"Seven in the morning?" she asked.

"First game's at nine. See you then," he said and leaned down and kissed her. "Good night, Julie," he said softly and turned and left.

As he drove home, Dallas replayed that kiss in his mind. It was just a peck, and he had wanted more, but he had reminded himself to take this relationship slow and easy. There was something very special about Julie.

He liked her family. They might go overboard when it came to sports, yet he instinctively knew that they loved and respected Julie. Somehow, she didn't see it.

"Dear God, how do we convince her of that?" Dallas turned to his usual way of problem solving and felt a sense of peace settle over him.

By Saturday, Julie was ready for an easy day. Her students were wild as the countdown to vacation neared its end. The last day of school would have been a total loss if she hadn't scheduled their in-class essays. As it was, she let them write for the first hour and led a discussion the second hour. By eleven o'clock, the tension was so high, it was hard to keep their attention. Julie switched the discussion to what they were going to do with the three weeks before the fall semester began.

"I'm working on the baseball committee," one of the football players said. "We had a meeting last night and decided students should be involved, too. Miss Russell, are you going to help Dallas Stone?" He looked at another student and grinned. "We saw you on the square with him the other night."

"I'm not sure how I feel about adding another sport to the curriculum," Julie answered stiffly and then changed the subject. "Our time is about up. I'll post your grades by your student numbers on Monday. Grades will be mailed on Tuesday, so if you can't drop by the office to see what you made, you should get them Wednesday. Are there any questions?"

No one held up a hand.

"In that case, let's take off ten minutes early. Enjoy the next three weeks."

She was glad she was standing behind her desk. It protected her from the stampede of students. By three o'clock her papers were graded. Another hour finished up the grade averaging.

On her way out of the school, she gave her official envelope to the secretary and thumbtacked her grade list to the bulletin board.

Free at last! She offered a prayer of gratitude and felt the exhilaration her students must have felt that morning. No cares, no worries, three whole weeks of nothing to do before school started again.

It was with the same high feeling that she greeted Dallas Stone at seven o'clock the next morning.

"You're in a great mood," he noted as he opened the car door for her.

"Yes," she said. "I feel terrific. 'God's in his heaven, all's right with the world,' " she quoted. She explained about her euphoric feeling after turning in her grades.

"Adrenaline was high," he said. "I know the feeling. It's like that when you've played a good game. You've got life by the tail and are swinging it around. Nothing can get you down."

"Exactly," she said. "Not that I don't like teaching. I love it. But this break is just what I need before starting again with more students."

Dallas pulled over at the truck stop at the edge of town.

"The more trucks, the better the food," he told Julie as they looked over the menus. "I like a big breakfast."

"I know," she said. At his raised eyebrows, she added, "I saw breakfast food in your refrigerator."

"It's the main meal of the day," he said.

When the food arrived, he reached across the table for her hand and held it, then silently bowed his head. A moment later he looked up into her smiling eyes. While he devoured bacon, eggs, biscuits and gravy, and hash browns, Julie ate an English muffin with blueberry jam.

"How was your meeting Thursday night?" Julie asked.

"Great. We're getting organized. There were about fifty people there, which is much too big for a committee. We elected seven people to serve on a board of directors. We meet again next week and hope to have our objectives on paper. We were going too many directions Thursday."

"Was John there?"

"Yes. Your dad was there, too."

"You're on the board?" she asked, but she knew it was a foregone conclusion.

Dallas nodded. "Chairman. I'll be making a lot of presentations to community groups as soon as we have all our facts together. Your brother-in-law is on the board, too."

"Wade is a good choice. What about Cindy? Were there any women elected?"

"Cindy was there. I don't believe there are any women on the board. Is that a problem?"

"Seems to me you would have a more rounded board if both genders were represented."

"You may be right. Will you serve as an ex officio member? You would have some insights into the teacher's side of the issue."

"I don't think I'd be a wise choice for this committee."

"All right," he said. He didn't want to push her. "It's after eight. We'd better move on if we're going to get to the park for the first game. "I've arranged for a car at the airport, but it's a fifteen minute drive from there to the ball field."

"We're flying?" Julie asked.

"Didn't I mention that?"

She shook her head.

"Sorry. Does it bother you? I'm a good pilot, but we can drive if you'd rather."

"No," she assured him and smiled. "I'm ready for a new adventure. I trust you." And she did. She trusted him on the ground and she trusted him in the air. She didn't want to analyze that feeling. It felt so natural, she wanted only to enjoy it.

In a very few minutes, Dallas had filed a flight plan and checked over his two-engine airplane. After a quick takeoff, they were airborne.

Although she had just assured Dallas that she trusted him, Julie silently said a quick prayer for their safety as she looked down at the town below them. She picked out landmarks that grew smaller and smaller as the plane climbed.

"This is quite an airplane. How many can it carry?"

"Oh, six or seven. I wanted to be able to take friends with me wherever I went, so I bought a big one."

"You own this?"

"I received large bonuses during my playing career. This is one of them. Look down there. That's Lamar."

Julie watched the miniature town with Matchbox cars. Quickly the landscape changed to the pattern fields of soybeans, corn, and wheat, broken by an occasional farmhouse and other small towns. *How wonderful was God's creation,* Julie thought. She was fascinated by the view and was surprised when Dallas radioed the airport to ask for clearance to land.

"We're already there?"

"Doesn't take long when you fly. Besides the feeling of absolute freedom, the time factor is a real plus for flying."

They made it to the park in time to see the first ball thrown out.

"When does Gentry play?" Julie asked.

"Around eleven. They follow this game on this same

field," Dallas replied after consulting the tournament brackets posted on the concession stand.

They found seats in the stands and Dallas turned to Julie. "There are a lot of positives about baseball," he started. "The player has to learn to be one of a team and yet do the very best that he can as an individual player."

"Have I heard this lecture before?"

Dallas chuckled. "You can't blame me for trying."

"I'm here, aren't I?"

"Yeah, that's a start. Who are you rooting for in this game? I'm for Jeff City."

"Then I will be, too."

Dallas explained the rules and the fine points of the game as the innings flew by.

"The pitcher will throw high, outside next," Dallas said.

"How do you know?"

"The batter swung at the last one. He'll throw it again."

"You mean he'll throw a ball on purpose?"

"Sure. You mix up the pitches. If you threw strikes all the time, they'd hit you out of the park."

"I always thought the pitchers were wild when they threw balls."

"That's true when they get tired and lose control, but they throw a mix to confuse the batter. Your brothers didn't teach you that?"

"I may not have listened if they ever tried," Julie admitted. Usually she blocked her brothers out when talk turned to sports.

"Well, you're learning now," Dallas said.

Julie had to admit it was a more exciting game if she

knew what was going on.

"Well, we won that one," Dallas said after the game was over and the Gentry team was taking infield practice. "Now for the big event. If Gentry wins, they'll play again this evening."

"I'm surprised Mel Cooney coaches, but I don't know him well. His classroom's in a different wing, so I rarely see him."

"He was elected to the baseball committee board." Dallas looked around and stood up. "We're on the wrong side of the stands. Let's move over. We need to get into the spirit of this game."

Surrounded by parents and friends of the Gentry team, Julie got into the spirit and rooted for the neighboring community's team.

"It doesn't get much better than this," Dallas said as he and Julie settled down again after a trip to the concession stand. "Hot dogs, Cokes, a sunny afternoon. And kids out there playing baseball."

"That was not a strike, ump," one parent yelled.

"The ump needs glasses," another chimed in.

Julie glanced at Dallas.

He shrugged. "Sometimes the fans get a little over zealous."

A Gentry player tried to steal home and got thrown out.

"He was safe," a mother screamed. "There was no way he was out." She started to climb down from the bleachers, but her husband held her back.

"They can't do that to us," she argued with her husband.

Her son threw his helmet into the dirt.

"That's when I'd jerk him out of the game," Dallas said. "Although I can see he gets the bad attitude from his mother. There's no room for that sort of behavior on a team." He turned his attention back to the game.

Julie studied Dallas. His eyes had narrowed to slits showing his displeasure with the Gentry team's sportsmanship. His lips had thinned to a straight line, and Julie wished his smile was back in place.

She knew those lips could be softer. She'd experienced their tenderness when he had given her that one brief kiss. What was she thinking! She quit staring at him and saw that Gentry's team was already back in the field.

The first two Columbia batters walked. A close play at first brought half the crowd to its feet. "He was out, ump," one fan yelled.

"We're getting bad calls," another shouted. "Did Columbia bring their own umpires?"

Mel Cooney walked out to the first base umpire and complained loudly. The umpire listened but did not reverse the call.

With bases loaded, the Gentry squad blew their chance for a double play as the short stop bobbled the ball. One run scored.

The next batter struck out, and the runner on third stole home on an overthrow.

The parents were on their feet yelling at their sons.

It didn't surprise Julie when Mel Cooney stormed up to the umpire after another close call on first.

The fans booed. Mel Cooney stood nose to nose with the first base umpire, expressing his views in a voice loud enough for Julie to hear. The players pressed against the wire of the dugout to watch the scene. Parents on both sides yelled and ran for the fence. Chaos erupted.

Left in the stands, Julie turned to Dallas. "What did you say about it not getting much better than this?"

# five

"You really don't mind Chinese food again so soon?" Dallas asked.

"It would be a shame to waste this opportunity," Julie replied. "Springfield has a Chinese restaurant on every corner. The problem is, how do we pick one?"

"The Dragon comes highly recommended," Dallas said and drove them straight to that restaurant.

They had watched the Gentry team be eliminated from the tournament. It was a wonder the team had not been ejected, but the umpires had restored order and the teams had completed the game. After that, Dallas had suggested they leave the ball fields and tour Springfield.

They had spent a couple of hours at the zoo, then gone to a mall. Julie gladly had traded the heat radiating from the sidewalks for the cool walkways at the shopping mall. Although neither one was shopping for anything in particular, they had enjoyed strolling along watching the people. Dallas had paid particular interest to the sporting goods store.

"Checking out the competition," he had told Julie.

Later, when they had reached the restaurant and had been served their food, conversation again turned to the Gentry game.

"You haven't said 'I told you so' or something close to that," Dallas commented as they dug into their moo goo gai pan.

"No need. You had nothing to do with that fiasco. Those parents started the whole mess by objecting to the umpires' decisions. The boys just followed suit. It's too bad, really. It's just a game," Julie said and waved her fork for emphasis. "My brothers have told me that sports build character. Not today."

Dallas studied Julie across the table. That morning she had seemed closer to understanding how important baseball was to him, but the Gentry game had only redefined her negative feelings instead of accenuating the positive aspects of the sport.

"You're right, but it's not always that way. It's hard to control the parents. They want their sons to excel, and they don't want their sons blamed when something goes wrong. That's a problem with society as a whole, not just in sports. No one wants to take responsibility when he's at fault."

"True. I've seen that at school, too. Sometimes parents come in and say I gave their child a grade. I quickly point out that their child earned a grade. Parents are reluctant to accept that."

Dallas laughed. "When I'm a parent, I may feel the same way. But I hope I'm smarter than that."

"Me, too. Dallas, about parents—I don't want you to feel obligated to go to Sunday dinner at my folks'. I have a large, sometimes meddling, family."

"Don't you want me to go?" His brow knit with concern.

"If you'd like to come," Julie said, which didn't reassure Dallas one bit.

"Would you like me to come?" he restated.

"Yes," she admitted. "You've met John, and he's moderately sane. But my other brothers are great teases. They delight in embarrassing me."

"The fifth degree? What are my intentions and all that?"

"Exactly."

"I think I can handle it," he said and grinned. "What time should I pick you up?"

"That depends. What time do you get out of church?"

"A little before noon. How about you?"

"I go to early service and then teach a Sunday school class, so I'm through by eleven."

"That explains why the only time I saw you at church was when your car was pulling out of the parking lot just as I was arriving. I've seen Cindy and Wade at the second service once in a while, but never you. And believe me, I would have remembered seeing you."

Julie smiled. "Because we have Sunday dinner, my whole family usually goes to early service. Then we have time to cook before noon."

"Shall we go together to early service then?"

"Okay. That sounds good."

Actually it sounded marvelous to Julie. There weren't that many eligible Christian men around, and she had enjoyed being with Dallas: walking beside him, holding hands, eating in an intimate booth that closed the rest of the world out.

Julie beamed at him. "Are there more baseball games this evening?" she asked.

Dallas nodded.

"Do we need to fly home before dark?"

"No. I have instrument rating."

"Then shall we go watch another game before we go home?" Julie suggested.

"Sure," he said, his eyes lighting up. "Are you going

to turn into a baseball fan after all?"

"I wouldn't bank on it, but I can compromise."

They watched another game and were back in the air on their way to Tribune by nine o'clock. Dallas watched the instruments and dials and Julie watched the lights of Springfield grow smaller. Before long there was nothing but darkness below them. A glow ahead claimed Julie's attention.

"What's that?"

"The ball field at Cantrell. Probably Little League."

"Ah," she murmured.

They flew over the field and on into darkness.

"Down there's Siloam," Dallas said as they approached another small town. Again, a round glow of lights greeted Julie.

"Another ball field?" Julie guessed.

"Yeah."

For the next half-hour they flew on an invisible road in the sky, led from small town to small town by lighted baseball parks. Julie strained her eyes, searching for the next one and the next one. They kept coming and kept coming, their lights resembling earthly halos.

"Quite impressive," she said softly. "I feel like I should be holding an apple pie and waving the flag."

"Exactly," Dallas said. "It is the favorite American pastime," he added and grinned.

Sooner than Dallas would have liked, he had landed the plane, driven Julie home, and was standing outside the door of her duplex wishing her good night. He gazed into her deep blue eyes and felt himself drowning. Gently, he kissed her lips, then traced the outline of her cheek with his hand.

"Thanks for a wonderful day," he whispered huskily. "Good night." He waited until Julie was safely inside her home, then walked to his car and left.

Dallas jerked his dark hair first one way, then another after he changed from slacks to jeans for casual Sunday dinner at the Russells'. He stood at the bathroom mirror and pulled a wet comb through his hair. It tended to curl when he wanted it to be perfectly straight, and it was too long. He should have seen a barber before having dinner with her family.

It was no use. He tossed the comb on the counter. This was just a family dinner. He had already met her parents and her brother John. He knew Wade and Cindy. So why was he as nervous as a sixteen-year-old on a first date?

"The unknown," he said out loud. "Merle and Tom. How bad could they be?" He had taken Julie's warning about her brothers to heart.

Most people were impressed by his pitching career. Especially baseball fans. Her family loved sports, so he had nothing to worry about. "But Julie's not impressed with an athlete," he told his image in the mirror.

As he drove over to Julie's, he nervously tapped his fingers on the steering wheel. He had dropped her off after Sunday school so she could change clothes. Then he had gone home to change himself.

He had liked sitting next to Julie in church, had liked sharing a hymn book. He had gone to her Sunday school class of fourth graders and sat in the back of the room with a perfect excuse for staring at her as she taught.

Her lesson had been based on Proverbs 12:15. "The way of a fool seems right to him, but a wise man listens to advice" (NIV). Dallas had listened carefully as Julie had drawn her students into a discussion and led them to the conclusion that they ought to listen to their parents and not let peer pressure rule their lives.

Each time a student had responded, she had given her undivided attention, as if the speaker were the only one in the room. He liked that in her. Actually, there was a lot he saw in her to like.

When he pulled into her driveway, she was waiting for him on her front step. Her blond hair was pulled back in a ponytail, much like it was the first day he had met her at the ballpark.

"Good news," she said, as she climbed into the car. "You have a reprieve of sorts."

"I do?"

"I just talked to Mom to see if she needed anything from town. She said Tom's brought home a girl from college, so he won't bother you a bit in the hope that I'll leave him alone."

"Sounds like such a wonderful sibling relationship."

Julie grinned. "I remember taking a boyfriend home from college several years ago and really wanting to impress him. Tom got me on the floor in a wrestling hold, and I thought I would never get up. I could have choked him."

"How old is Tom?"

"Twenty-one. He just finished summer school. He'll be a senior next year. This is the first time he's brought someone home to meet the family. He'll be on pins and needles the entire time," she said with a gleam in her eye.

Dallas drove down the long lane that led to the Russell

farm. The house sat away from an assortment of out-buildings, including a traditional red barn. Several cars were parked on the graveled area beside a detached garage.

"Looks like quite an operation here," he said.

"It was my grandfather's farm. Some of the buildings are outdated and aren't used anymore. The milk barn's empty. Mom and Dad raise beef cattle now. The smoke house is full of old furniture. My apartment was furnished out of there."

"Are we the last to arrive?"

"Looks like it. We'll get to make a grand entrance. Don't worry, they'll love having you. Just try to remember names. That will impress them."

Dallas did his best. He remembered John and easily associated his wife Tara with him. Their daughters, the three Ts, he confused. Merle and Linda were friendly, but they were busy chasing a two-year-old son and passing an infant between them. Tom looked as self-conscious as Dallas felt. His girlfriend, Elaine, was pretty, and stayed beside Tom every moment.

Dallas hung around Wade and Cindy. He already knew them because their son had played on his team and he felt more at ease with them.

"I need help in the kitchen," Evelyn Russell announced to her daughters.

"Can...uh...May I help?" Dallas asked.

"Noooo," Charles Russell said and put his arm around Dallas's shoulders. "You stick with the men folk in here."

Dallas glanced at Julie and saw the tight line of her lips as she went into the kitchen. Dallas wanted to follow her, but he didn't think he should alienate Julie's father on a first visit to his home.

Mr. Russell led Dallas to one end of the long living room.

"Evelyn got tired of dusting trophies, so I made her a trophy case," he said proudly.

"That's quite a collection." Dallas had never seen so many trophies in a private home.

"And it's not all of them. The boys and Cindy have taken a few of them to their homes. Of course, a lot of these are mine, because of coaching Little League teams."

Dallas admired the trophies and the workmanship of the glass-fronted case, then turned and saw Julie in the doorway between the kitchen and living room. She nodded as if understanding something that escaped his knowledge.

"I see Dad's entertaining you."

"We're doing just fine," Charles Russell informed his daughter.

Julie gave Dallas a weak smile and popped back into the kitchen.

During the next half-hour, Dallas answered questions about his pro career. Julie would glance into the room every now and then, and each time Dallas saw her, he would flash a smile to assure her that he was having a good time. What he really wanted was to be with her, but surely after dinner he'd have that opportunity.

"Dinner," Evelyn Russell finally announced. Dallas followed the men into the huge country kitchen and stood behind Julie while Mr. Russell asked the group for quiet.

"Our heavenly Father, thank You for this wonderful food we are about to eat. We ask that You nourish it to our bodies and make them strong. Thank You for letting Dallas and Elaine join us today. Please help us make them welcome in our home. In Jesus' name, Amen."

The adults echoed, "Amen."

The kids filed around the food-laden table with their parents helping the younger ones fill their plates. Charles, his sons, Wade, and Dallas went through next, followed by the women.

After dinner, the men lounged in front of the television watching a baseball game. Dallas entertained them with a few personal anecdotes about some of the players. From the kitchen came the sounds of rattling plates and silverware. Dallas kept glancing toward the kitchen but didn't buck the Russell ritual.

The doorbell rang and John answered it.

"Why, Tennis! When did you get in?"

"This morning," the man said as he shook hands with John. "Where's Julie?"

"In the kitchen."

The newcomer started in that direction, but Charles stood up and offered his hand.

"Welcome home, Tennis."

Tennis shook hands with Charles and then Merle before Julie burst into the room, followed by John.

"Tennis," she said and hugged him. It wasn't just a hug. He swung her around. Twice.

"Who's Tennis? A tennis player?" Dallas asked Merle, who had returned to his seat beside him on the couch.

"Nope. Tennis was named after his grandfather. He

grew up on the farm next door. He and Julie have been friends forever."

Dallas felt uncomfortable. The other women had filed into the living room. Everyone seemed to have forgotten that he had come with Julie. Certainly Julie had forgotten it. She was still standing by Tennis.

Dallas studied him as he addressed each of the Russells. He had no trouble with so many names. He was tall, but Dallas figured his own six–feet–two had him by at least an inch. Tennis was wearing cutoffs and a white golf shirt. His blond hair matched the golden color of Julie's.

Tennis shook hands with Tom. Then it was Dallas's turn.

"Dallas," Julie said. "This is my very good friend, Tennis Begee." The two men shook hands.

"Tennis just finished his doctorate at Princeton," Julie bragged. "In English lit. How long will you be in town, Tennis?"

Dallas was interested in the answer, too.

"Two weeks. Then off to UCLA."

"That's so exciting," Julie said. "A teaching job at a big school like that. What about your book? He's written a wonderful critical work on Harold Pinter," she explained to Dallas. "When's it due out?"

"I have an advance copy for you in the car," Tennis said.

"Oh, let me see it. Have you signed it?"

"Not yet. I'll get it for you pretty soon." He walked with the women toward the kitchen.

Dallas stood up to follow them, but Charles asked him if he knew another ballplayer on television. A lengthy discussion followed. Before Dallas had another opportunity to join the women in the kitchen, they returned en masse to the living room.

Julie walked over to Dallas and sat down beside him. He stretched his arm out along the couch behind her.

"Are you getting along okay in here?" she whispered to him.

"Okay," he whispered back, liking the intimacy of their private conversation in the midst of the group.

"Dallas," Tom said, "I understand you're organizing a group to get a baseball team for the high school. Sure wish we'd had one when I went to school."

"We're in the planning stages and can use any help you can give us," Dallas answered.

"Do you have a budget outlined?" Tom asked.

"We've started itemizing expenses. Uniforms, equipment, coaches' salaries, bus transportation, insurance."

"What about a stadium?" Tom asked.

"We're going to rent the American Legion ball field," John answered, jumping into the conversation. "We'll maintain it with volunteers, but we'll still need access to mowers. We haven't gotten far enough to know if we should buy them or if we can pay the Legion for the use of the ones in the utility shed."

"This here a committee meeting?" Charles demanded from his recliner.

"We can use input anytime we can get it," Dallas said. "There's a lot to maintaining a ball field. Sometimes it needs new sod. We have to have marble dust to chalk the foul lines. After a rain we'll need Quick-Dry to get the field ready for a game. We should make a list of every item we're going to need and a liberal estimate of how much."

Wade joined the discussion. "Where's a pencil and paper, Evelyn?" he asked his wife's mother.

"Okay, shoot," he said once he had a pen ready.

Dallas reiterated the expenses.

"What about utilities? Lights for night games, water for the concession stand and the bathrooms," Tom said.

"The concession stand should be a real money maker if it's handled right," Cindy inserted. "Canisters of soft drinks make big bucks. Add a little extra salt to the popcorn and drinks sell very well."

"Julie pointed out to me yesterday that we have no women on the baseball committee. I'm not trying to sound sexist," Dallas said to Julie, "but I think women are more knowledgeable about concession stands than men. We need someone to head up that area. Interested, Cindy?"

"It does sound sexist," Cindy said. "But, why not? I know other mothers and some fathers who would be glad to help out if they don't have to work too many times. How many games are we talking about, Dallas?"

"I'm not sure. How many area towns have teams?"

"Gentry," Julie said and shook her head, remembering yesterday's chaotic game.

She got up from the couch and walked over to where Tennis leaned against the wall. She said something to him that Dallas couldn't hear over the din of the Russell men naming surrounding communities which had high school baseball teams. Dallas watched in dismay as Julie disappeared with Tennis into the kitchen.

"I believe a school only plays other schools with the same classification," John said. "Triple A schools don't play bigger Five A schools."

"He's right," Merle said. "We'd play the same scho
that we do in basketball and football. Maybe we co
play other schools in nonconference games."

"There are ten schools in the conference," Tom sa

"Then we'd play each one twice," Dallas said. "Pro
ably double-headers with the schools that are so
distance away."

"How about some homemade ice cream, Evelyn
Charles's big voice boomed out.

Evelyn smiled and nodded. "I'll need some cranker
she said. "Jimmie," she called to her grandson. "Get fe
jugs of ice from the deep freeze and bust them up," s
said as she got up and headed to the kitchen. Dal
followed her into the woman's domain and found Ju
and Tennis deep in conversation at the kitchen table.

"I'm sure they have course outlines for the lit clas:
so the entire department is in sync. But with the Pin
seminar, I'll be my own boss," Tennis was telling Jul

Dallas walked over by Julie and placed his hand on I
shoulder. "We're having homemade ice cream
haven't had any in ages."

Julie got eggs out of the refrigerator and Evelyn beg
mixing a concoction without benefit of a written reci;
All the while, Julie's conversation with Tennis conce
ing syllabi and course requirements continued, eff
tively blocking Dallas from the discussion.

The group in the living room drifted outside to 1
well house when the ice cream mixture was ready to
cranked in the ice cream maker.

Dallas helped Jimmie break up big chunks of ice tl
had been frozen in gallon milk cartons.

"Add more salt to the ice," Merle said as he took his turn at the handle. "It's melting pretty good now."

When the paddles could be turned no longer, John pulled them out of the ice cream drum, packed the maker with ice, and covered the top with brown grocery sacks.

"Let's give it an hour," he said and looked at his watch.

The family lazed around in metal lawn chairs and on the ground under the shade of a couple of huge oaks. Julie sat between Dallas and Tennis. Several conversations transpired at the same time.

"Just what are your intentions toward my sister?" Merle asked Dallas as he sat leaning back in his chair.

Dallas laughed and glanced at Julie who was turning an interesting shade of pink. "Julie warned me you'd ask that."

"Well?"

"I don't know yet. Today I'm just here to check out the family—see if there are any disreputable types."

Merle sat up straight, the front part of his chair hitting the ground with a soft thump.

"Rarely have I seen Merle at a loss for words," Julie said. "Thanks, Dallas. I've waited a long time for this."

Merle laughed. "You're good, Dallas."

"Julie, would you walk me out to the car," Tennis asked suddenly.

Dallas watched them walk away again. This day was not going as he had planned. He stared after them and saw Tennis reach into the car and hand a book to Julie.

She opened the volume and squealed, then hugged Tennis.

"Can you imagine?" she said as she joined the family

under the trees. She read the dedication aloud. "For my family for their encouragement and to Julie, who always believed in me."

## six

Julie helped dish up the ice cream. "Want some chocolate on top, Tennis?" she asked her friend. She was delighted to see him again. He hadn't returned over the Christmas holiday, so it had been a full year since his last trip home.

He was like a brother to her. Her own brothers were jocks and teased her for being a girl. Tennis had shared the things that were important to her. They were kindred spirits.

"Dallas, what kind of topping would you like?" Julie asked.

"Chocolate will be fine, thank you," he said formally. He didn't step toward her, but kept his distance.

Where before he had appeared to be enjoying her family, he now seemed distant, even remote. Julie glared suspiciously at Merle, wondering if he had started teasing Dallas while she was inside getting the dishes.

Dallas took his ice cream and walked over to lean against an oak tree. Tennis came up beside him.

"John tells me you're here with Julie," he said with a smile. "We're good friends."

"Oh," Dallas said as if whether they were or weren't didn't matter one bit. But inside he winced.

"Dallas Stone. Chicago White Sox. I should have recognized you immediately. I'd heard you'd opened a store here."

"I'm a retired player now. I moved to Tribune several

months ago."

"I remember the news of your accident. I figured you'd land on your feet. The articles I read about you gave the impression you were a sensible fellow."

Dallas ate a bite of ice cream. He wasn't sure how to respond to being called a sensible fellow. He wished Tennis would go away. No matter how many times he was told that Tennis and Julie were just good friends, and John and Evelyn had both said that same phrase to him, he'd never believe it. Julie was beaming and couldn't keep her eyes off Tennis.

Dallas downed the last of his ice cream and carried the empty bowl to the kitchen where Julie was washing dishes. He plunked his bowl down on the counter, picked up a dish towel, and began drying spoons and bowls. Julie pointed out the silverware drawer, and he placed the clean spoons inside.

"You don't need to help," she said.

*Sure I don't,* Dallas thought. Julie had allowed Tennis in the kitchen, and Dallas was going to make sure that she allowed him as well. Although she hadn't said so in words, her feelings toward the male-dominated household were obvious. He was determined to show her that he could be as sensitive to her feelings as the next guy, and in this case, the next guy was Tennis.

Others brought dishes in, and they continued to work until they had the dishes caught up.

"Thanks," Julie said. "Are you ready to go?"

"Yes," Dallas said bluntly without making up an excuse.

"Give me a minute to get my purse."

Dallas thanked the Russells for dinner and told Julie's

siblings he would be talking to them again about the committee. He had tucked Wade's list in his shirt pocket and would use it for reference when the board met to draw up a budget.

"Julie, I'll call you," Tennis told her as they said their goodbyes.

Julie hugged him again. "I'm so glad you're home. Perfect timing, too. I'm on vacation for three weeks."

"I hope you didn't find my family too annoying," Julie said to Dallas once they were in the privacy of his car. Dallas was unnaturally quiet. "I thought they were pretty well behaved for them."

"Who was it that Tennis wrote about?" he asked.

"Harold Pinter," she said. "The playwright."

"His work is interesting," Dallas said, although he'd never heard of the man.

"I'm glad you like Pinter," Julie said, jumping to a conclusion Dallas didn't correct. "I'm sure Tennis would like to hear your opinions. While he's home, maybe we can barbecue out or something."

"Sure," Dallas said.

"When is the next committee meeting?" Julie asked, trying to draw Dallas out of his mood.

"The board meets tomorrow night. We report back to the whole committee on Thursday," he replied in clipped tones. He turned into her driveway.

"I'll tell Tennis when he calls, in case he's interested. He's always liked baseball, even though he never played."

*He's just an all around guy,* Dallas thought gloomily as he walked Julie to her door.

"Thanks for coming with me today," she said. "They

liked you."

Dallas leaned down and kissed her on the lips. He pulled her closer and she didn't resist, but leaned toward him as he kissed her again.

*I'll bet Tennis doesn't kiss her like this,* he thought.

"I'll call you," he said. As soon as he'd said it, he remembered that Tennis had said the same thing.


"What time does the library open?" Dallas asked his business partner.

"Nine, I think," Alex said.

"Who's Harold Pinter?"

"Never heard of him. Is he a rookie?"

"No. He's a playwright. We're Monday morning slow. Mind if I run downtown?"

"Go on. I can manage here."

Within minutes, Dallas pulled into a parking space at the library. He felt bad about giving Julie the wrong impression. Actually, he had lied, he had to admit.

"Forgive me, Lord," he breathed. "I'll straighten it out with her."

Meanwhile he intended to find out what he could about Harold Pinter.

"We have a few of his plays," the librarian said, "and I remember an older volume about him, maybe twenty years old. I'll bet we can find more current information in magazines."

She helped him locate two literary magazines. Dallas left the library with a brief biography and a volume of six plays.

"Does this Pinter guy have anything to do with Julie Russell?" Alex asked Dallas, who had been studying the books half the day. He leaned in the doorway to Dallas's office and studied his partner.

"A little," Dallas replied noncommittally.

"You ought to ask Tennis Begee about him. He's back in town and has a doctorate in English from Duke."

"English literature from Princeton. He's written a book about Pinter."

"Whatever," Alex said and laughed. "Julie Russell and Tennis Begee are good friends," he said. "They grew up on neighboring farms. Is that what this is all about?"

"How do you know so much about them?"

"In a town of nine thousand people, you get to know quite a few if you've lived here as long as I have. Even though I worked out of town until you started this store, I've lived here for twenty years and have grown kids who went to school with the Russells—and the Begees, for that matter. You've only been here months. Wait a couple of years and we'll see how many people you know."

"What else do you know about Julie Russell?" Dallas didn't have any qualms about asking questions. He wanted to know anything about her that would give him ammunition to use against a man he saw as a threat.

"Julie's always been brainy. She was valedictorian of her senior class. Tennis is a year older than she is and he was valedictorian of his class. That the kind of thing you want to know?"

"Keep going."

"Well, they're friends. Don't know that I ever knew them to be more than that. I don't remember Julie going out a lot in high school. Boys were afraid of her. She was too smart. Tennis was a nice boy. He and my son were pretty good friends."

"Anything you don't like about Tennis?"

"Nope. Everybody likes Tennis. Julie was always his special friend, though."

"What about Julie in college? Know anything about those years?" Dallas pushed out his chair and stood up.

"A little. I know she was homecoming queen one year. It was in the papers, and it was a joke around here about her going with some basketball player. You know, her being so short and not being a sports fan. It never came to anything, she and the basketball player. Now that I think about it, she's always been around tall guys. Tennis is about your size."

"He's at least an inch shorter," Dallas said defensively.

"Uh-huh. Seems to me you might have a problem on your hands."

"I thought you said they were just friends?"

"I did. Doesn't help the little green monster, though, does it?"

"Jealous? You think I'm jealous of Tennis Begee?"

"Nope. I think you're jealous of his relationship with Julie Russell."

Dallas closed his eyes and looked inward. *I don't want to be jealous, Lord. I just want Julie to care specially for me, not Tennis.* He opened his eyes to see Alex studying him. His partner opened his mouth to say something, seemed to think better of it, then shifted the conversation. "I came in here to ask if you wanted to go ahead and order some red baseball caps that say Tribune High School. Seems like a few of those around might be a money maker for the committee."

"Alex, you've got something there. People wearing them around would be good publicity for the committee, too. But what about conflict of interest?"

"Simple. There is none. We order caps and sell them to the committee at cost. Then they jack up the price and the profit goes to the team fund. We don't see any money. We're just the ones who have access to the order blank."

"You're brilliant, Alex. Let's hold off a day. I'll present your idea to the board tonight." He sat down behind his desk. "Do you need any help on the floor? I should type up this list of budget items before the meeting."

"Slow day. Have you got red licorice on the list for the concession stand? It's a big seller."

"And your favorite. I'll make sure it gets on the list," Dallas said. He stacked his Pinter books and settled down to work on the budget, determinedly pushing thoughts of Julie to the back of his mind. Alex ambled back into the store as the bell above the door announced a customer.

Dallas looked through the glass wall to see Julie walking toward his office. He quickly stashed the Pinter books in the bottom drawer of his desk.

Julie had hovered outside the store for several minutes before she had found the courage to walk in. Something had gone desperately wrong on Sunday, and she wanted things right between herself and Dallas.

Oh, their day had started great. Sitting with Dallas in church had given her a wonderful feeling of spiritual blending. The church meant a lot to her, and he was a part of it.

Their Sunday together had ended great too, with those special kisses. On that score she had no complaint. A definite chemistry existed between them.

But somewhere in the middle of their day, things had gone very wrong. If she could fix it, she would. She walked toward him.

"Julie," Dallas said, meeting her at the office door. "This is a pleasant surprise."

"I was in the neighborhood," she said and laughed nervously. "Actually, I was. I needed a new computer ribbon from next door." She looked around the store. "This is my first time in here."

"Let me give you the fifty-cent tour," Dallas said. He casually linked her arm through his and strolled with her through the aisles of sweatshirts, tee shirts, football jerseys, running shoes, footballs, and trophies.

"As you can see, we're ready for the fall season. The retail business is always a season ahead."

"I've always wondered about that," Julie said. "I'm the type that wants to buy a swim suit in July, not in February when mannequins are wearing them."

"Back here is the store room. We also have storage above us on a mezzanine level."

"This is Alex's office?" she asked. It was smaller than Dallas's and near the back, away from the main sales floor.

"Yes. He says when he wants to be in there, he wants to be alone. Mine's up here."

He walked her to the glass enclosed space. "I wanted to be visible to the public." The minute he said that, he knew he had phrased it wrong.

"I see. The baseball star as a drawing card."

"Something like that. But, I also wanted to be able to see the customers and be able to help if needed." He didn't like to admit that she had accurately assessed his glass office. He and Alex had decided that a high profile for the former Chicago pitcher would be good for business.

"I guess I'd better go," Julie said. Things hadn't worked out. They seemed as tense together as they had been yesterday.

"We take breaks at the cafe. Do you have time for a cold drink?"

Julie hesitated.

"Julie, please. We need to talk."

Julie let him escort her to the cafe a few businesses down from his store and waited until the waitress had brought them each a cherry-limeade.

"You wanted to talk, Dallas?" *Please, God, don't let him say it's over between us before it's even begun.*

"What happened yesterday? I thought I was doing everything right. Your family seemed to like me okay."

"They liked you fine. Actually, you fit into my family better than I do."

"I thought you wanted me to fit in."

"Yes, I do. But you seemed just like them." She fiddled with her napkin, shredding it as they talked.

"Just like a real sports fan."

"Exactly."

"They are quite a crew. But they love you, Julie. They don't see you as second best because you aren't sports minded." He had given it a lot of thought and had decided the Russell family just didn't understand Julie.

Julie sat her glass down hard.

"They don't see value in nonathletes," she stated. "I've been trying for years to come to grips with it. I know God doesn't want families to quarrel. And my family believes that, too. So, mostly we avoid talking about my nonathletic ability."

"And avoid your intellectual ability, too. Perhaps they don't know how to talk to you. Compromise. You need to see the value of sports and your family needs to see the value of academics." He vowed to pray about it.

Julie nodded, but didn't say anything.

"So that's why you ignored me."

"I ignored you?" Julie picked up the pieces of her napkin and put them in the ash tray.

"Yes, you did. You and Tennis acted as if you wanted to be alone."

"I hadn't seen Tennis in a year. We're the best of friends. We're alike in ways my brothers and I could never be." She heaved a sigh and pushed wisps of hair back from her face. "I didn't realize I ignored you. I'm sorry if that's how it seemed."

"Apology accepted. I'm sorry I fit into your family."

Julie smiled. "You shouldn't feel sorry about that. I really wanted you to like them. I may not act like it, but my family is very important to me."

"I know. And you're important to them." At her disbelieving look, he added, "You are. You just don't recognized their ways of showing it." He took the lime out of his empty glass and ate a section.

"Well, I'm glad we got that settled. What have you been doing on your first Monday of vacation?" he asked to lighten their conversation.

"Relaxing," Julie said.

"You needed a computer ribbon to relax?" Dallas asked Julie.

"I'm going to type up a syllabus for my English lit class. And one for my basic English class, too."

"You call that a vacation?" he said and grinned.

"Getting prepared for school is different from teaching all day. I'm doing it very slowly. Does that count?"

"I'm going to have to teach you about relaxing," he said.

"Oh, that reminds me. Would you like to go hear the symphony in Joplin? The college is getting the St. Louis Symphony, and they are really good."

"Relaxing reminds you of the symphony?"

"Sure. Some of their music is very soothing. Anyway, Tom is going back to Joplin tomorrow, and he'll pick up tickets if we want to go."

"When is it?"

"Two weeks from Friday, right before school starts."

"Sounds fine," Dallas said and tried to muster some enthusiasm. He'd never heard a live symphony. Occasionally he would pass a classical station while tuning the car radio. That sort of music made him nervous. "We'll fly to Joplin," he added.

"Great. I know you'll enjoy it. Did you hear the Chicago Symphony when you lived there?"

"Ah, no," he admitted. "You know how it is. People who live in a city don't take advantage of all the events that tourists love."

"Yes, I know that's true. Dallas, thanks for the drink and the talk. I'm headed over to Linda and Merle's house. Linda's exhausted. The baby's not sleeping well at night, and during the day, Linda has a preschooler to chase. It's just a matter of time before things work out and they all adjust. I'm going to take little Joe off her hands for the rest of the afternoon. Maybe she can get a few minutes sleep while he's gone."

Julie took a final sip of her drink.

"I should be getting back, too. My partner might need me. Alex is the brains behind The Sports World. I'm learning the business from him."

Julie smiled and it made her face glow. So she liked humility. He could be as humble as the next guy.

"Thanks again for the drink, Dallas." She glanced at her watch. "I'd better move on if I want to pick up Joe."

"Tonight's the committee board meeting, but I'm free tomorrow night. Would you like to take in a movie?"

"Oh, thanks, Dallas, but I'm going to dinner at the Begees' tomorrow night. Tennis is only home for a couple of weeks. I'd like to spend as much time with him as I can." She looked him straight in the eyes and said, "But please understand. Tennis and I are just friends."

"Yes. I'll keep that in mind."

He walked her outside to her car and in broad daylight, in front of anyone in Tribune who happened to be passing by, he kissed her. Twice.

"I'll see you," he said and walked with a light step back to his store.

## seven

Dallas had not anticipated the large turnout for the board meeting. He had thought the seven members and Cindy would show up at the electric company's meeting room. Instead, there were at least thirty extra people.

"They think it's like the school board," Wade explained to Dallas. "Anybody can go listen to their meetings."

Dallas nodded and shuffled his papers in front of him. Playing baseball in front of thousands of fans and millions of television viewers hadn't bothered him, but standing in front of a group of people with their eyes glued expectantly on him made his hands grow clammy. Even his knees were shaking.

*Please God, help me do my best. And,* he added with an inward smile, *Help me not to not make a complete fool of myself.*

At seven o'clock sharp, Dallas started the meeting. Two hours later found him driving home, reviewing the meeting. They hadn't decided a lot during those two hours, but by Thursday the board members should have more information to give to the committee as a whole.

Dallas was only a few blocks from Julie's duplex and without consciously making the decision, he steered the car onto her street. Lights were on, but the drapes were pulled, so he couldn't see inside her home.

Impulsively, he parked in her driveway and walked to the door. He was keyed up about the meeting and wanted to tell her about it. He would ask her about using the school name on the baseball caps they wanted to sell as a fund-raiser.

Tennis answered his knock.

"Hello, Dallas. Come in," he said as if he owned the place.

"I didn't see your car," Dallas said.

"I let my little sister borrow it. She dropped me off here. Come in. Julie's in the kitchen. We got hungry."

Dallas knew he should leave, but he couldn't. He followed Tennis into the duplex. He had never been inside. Julie had always met him at the door or had been waiting on the steps for him to pick her up.

He looked around as Tennis led him through the living room. It wasn't large, but it was homey. A bookcase made of masonry blocks and wooden shelves covered one wall. Interspersed with books were pictures. A stereo system sat on a similar bookshelf on another wall. A small TV sat on a table in one corner. A couch and two mismatched chairs made up a conversation area.

"Hi, Dallas," Julie said from the kitchen doorway. "Come on in and have a seat."

He followed Tennis and sat down at the round table that dominated the dining area at one end of the kitchen.

"We're having baked potatoes. Want one?" Julie asked, as she went back to grating cheese.

"Sure," he said, although he wasn't hungry. It gave him an excuse to stay.

Julie washed a potato, stuck holes in it with a fork, and tossed it into the microwave. "Be just a few minutes."

Tennis had gone back to chopping a tomato. "I think I'd like some onion. How about you?" he asked.

"I'll pass," Julie answered quickly.

"Not for me," Dallas said. "Is there something I can do?"

"No, just talk to us. How was the board meeting?"

Dallas explained about all the extra people.

"That's a good sign. Means they're serious about this," Tennis said.

Dallas nodded. "As a kickoff, we discussed ordering ball caps with Tribune High School printed on them. Do you think the school would have an objection, Julie?"

"I don't see why. You'd have to ask the administration just to be sure. Mr. Kellough, our principal, is an ex-coach, so I hardly think he'd object."

The microwave dinged. Julie turned Dallas's potato over and added two others to rewarm. In a few minutes, the three sat down to add toppings to their potatoes.

"What we need is some crumbled bacon," Tennis said.

"Sorry, I'm out," Julie said.

"How about some mushrooms?" he asked.

"No."

"How about anchovies?"

"Tennis!" she exclaimed. "These are baked potatoes, not pizzas."

"Remember when we made that deluxe pizza for my family," Tennis said. "We put everything on it we could find in the refrigerator," he explained to Dallas. "Left-over roast beef, bologna cut up in strips—"

"And fresh spinach. Your mom had just picked it, and we thought it would work as well as green pepper. It didn't," Julie admitted and laughed. "We were just kids. Eight and nine?" She looked at Tennis for verification.

"Something like that."

"You've been friends for a long time," Dallas said. Even though Julie had assured him they were only friends, he had been watching them carefully, looking for secret glances, but had seen none.

"A long time," Tennis said. "And always will be. Julie made me go to Princeton. We had talked about it, but of course, it was too expensive. They charged fifty dollars just to apply. To make a long story short, Julie sent in the application for me, including the fifty dollars she'd earned baby-sitting. I was stunned to get not only the acceptance letter, but notification that I had a full scholarship as well. Of course there was no way I could pass that up."

"And the rest is history," Julie said modestly.

"No wonder you dedicated your book to Julie," Dallas said.

"I owe her a lot," Tennis said. "Say, Julie tells me you're interested in Harold Pinter's work."

"I don't know all that much about him," Dallas said. "But I am fascinated by his style. Without his pregnant pauses, his plays would be half as long as they are," he quoted from his morning's reading.

"That's one of his trademarks. Have you seen many of his productions?"

"I'm more familiar with his screenplays. *The French Lieutenant's Woman* is one of my favorites."

"Certainly it's his most well-known, but not his most award-winning film. I'm thinking of writing a book about his films and his career as a screenwriter. Of course, most of his movies are based on his plays, but some are original screenplays."

"That was a delicious potato," Dallas said, changing the subject. He had exhausted his limited knowledge about Pinter and he didn't want to get in too deep. Besides guilt was beginning to take over. He knew he should tell Julie that he hadn't heard of Pinter until Sunday. This didn't seem to be the moment, but he would tell her.

"Thanks. I really must be going. I just dropped by to get your opinion about the ball caps." He carried his plate to the sink.

"I'm glad you stopped by," Julie said. "Why don't you come over for a barbecue on Friday. I'll see if I can round up another couple. I'm sure Tennis can find a date. The grapevine's been busy. I've heard over and over that 'Tennis Begee's back in town.' You're in such demand," she teased her friend.

"That sounds great," Dallas said. Julie walked him to the door and lifted her head for him to kiss her.

Dallas almost skipped out to his car. He had met the enemy head-on and discovered Tennis wasn't an enemy at all. He might even become a friend.

"Thank you, thank you," he said as he lifted his eyes to the night sky.

*When you don't have all the facts, you make snap judgments that could be wrong and cause a lot of pain,* he thought. He remembered Julie's Sunday school lesson. "The way of a fool seems right to him, but a wise man listens to advice." Many times in his life he'd studied a particular verse and within the next few days been able to apply the words to his own life. This lesson was no exception. He should have heeded the Russells when they had told him that Julie and Tennis were only friends.

Well, now he knew there was no man in her life. Except him. And maybe an old college basketball player that Alex had mentioned.

*No,* he told himself. *You're doing it again. Get facts, don't dream up scenarios.*


Julie had worked hard getting her barbecue organized. She had included one other couple besides herself and Dallas and Tennis and his date, Lisa.

Folding chairs from the smokehouse storage room at her folks' were scattered on the patio. Tennis had helped her haul them to her duplex.

"What we need now," Tennis said as he plopped down on a chair, "is a big glass of iced tea—with lemon. Got any made?"

"Two jugs in the refrigerator. Bring me one, please."

Julie continued to carry plants to the patio. There was not enough room in her apartment for six people to sit around the table. She was determined to make the patio into a room of its own, like an outdoor cafe.

She had three wooden spools that had previously held electric wire to serve as tables. Tennis had cut old plywood from his father's woodworking shop into round disks that fit on the tops to make level eating surfaces. Each couple would have an individual table, yet be close enough to carry on conversations with the others.

Julie had retrieved some old kitchen curtains out of a storage box in the smokehouse and made three round tablecloths. The flowery design added to the look she was trying to achieve.

"Here," Tennis said and set two drinks on one table.

"Not on the table. They'll sweat and make rings on the tablecloths." She straightened one cloth so it hung evenly.

"You mean we're not going to eat off these tables? They're just for looks?"

"Of course we'll eat off them. But I want them fresh for this evening. What do you think? Should I put a plant in each corner or group them?" She stood back, trying to visualize the effect.

"How about one here and the others over there," he said and pointed to the edge of the patio.

Julie moved the fern, her biggest plant, by itself. The others were too scrawny to look good alone. "That's better." She took a chair and picked up her iced tea from the concrete slab where Tennis had moved it.

"What time is it? I've got to cook some of the chicken early. My grill's too small to hold it all at once."

"Almost three. You're sure doing this up in grand style. Everybody would have been happy with wieners on sticks."

"I want it to be special."

"I know. And yet you haven't said two words about Dallas. This is old Tennis, remember. Let's hear it."

"There's nothing to tell. We've been seeing each other some." *How can I tell Tennis that I've met a Christian man whose kisses set me on fire?* she asked herself.

"Enough for him to go to Sunday dinner."

"Dad invited him, not me. He's impressed with the big baseball star."

"And that bothers you, doesn't it?"

"No," Julie said and shook her head. "Well, yes. What

do you think of when I mention Bobby Lee?"

"Running the football back from kickoff. That was an eighty-seven–yard touchdown."

"Did you see it?" she questioned, although she already knew the answer.

"No. Bobby Lee is five, maybe six years older than I."

"Right. You didn't see it, but that's what you associate with Bobby Lee. He's been living on that story for years now. He can't move away because he has to be here where some people remember his glory days. He's been selling used cars and remembering the past."

"Does this somehow relate to Dallas?"

"A former baseball star? What do you think?" She repositioned the rubber band holding her ponytail to catch stray wisps of hair.

"Has he ever brought that up to you?"

"He told me about his accident and how much he missed baseball."

"That says a lot. I remember when he was hurt. He wouldn't talk to reporters after his accident. I'll bet not many people know how he feels about being out of baseball at the peak of his career." Tennis took a long drink of tea.

"Not only that," Tennis added, "but he's in Tribune. He didn't return to his hometown. He opened up a sporting goods store because that's in his field of expertise. Julie, as far as I can see Dallas is a fine Christian man. You've got to give the guy a chance and not hold sports against him."

"I'm not. I would just like to see him in other surroundings. I've been to baseball games and parties with him. And church and Sunday dinner," she added.

"And here at your house, discussing Harold Pinter. The guy is not stupid, Julie. Out of curiosity I stopped by that committee meeting last night. You ought to have seen him. He ran that meeting like a tight ship. When discussion on one topic ran too long, he ended it. He's a decision maker. A businessman. Don't sell him short because of your feelings toward athletes."

"I'm not. I know sports aren't his whole life. Did you know he's a pilot? I'd like to know his other interests, too."

"Other interests. Now that's an avenue to pursue. Do you know if Dallas had any other female interests before you entered the scene?"

"No. I don't want to think about that!" she said with vehemence.

Tennis leaned back in his chair and laughed.

# eight

The party was going well. The dinner had tasted great, and everyone appeared to be having a good time. Night had fallen and the only light on the patio was what poured out the kitchen window. Several conversations had been carried on at the same time until someone asked about the baseball committee.

*Not again,* Julie thought.

Carol, who taught algebra, immediately questioned the need of another sport at the high school. Although Julie agreed, she remained silent. Dallas already knew her views.

Lisa, Tennis's date, thought it was a good idea. Tennis kept quiet.

"We could give the games air time," Norm said. He worked at the radio station and was Carol's husband.

"That would be great," Dallas said and slipped his arm around Julie's chair to balance himself as he leaned back in his own. "We need to keep community involvement after we get the team on its feet. I'm hoping that charging admission to the games will allow us to stay in the black. We may not have to ask the school district for funds, even after three years."

"No new taxes," Norm said. "Seems like I've heard that before." The group laughed.

"That's one of the main planks in our platform," Dallas said. "This team can't cost the taxpayers a cent in the form of a new levy for the school system."

"Too bad the American Legion season is over already," Norm said. "A few games might draw attention to our cause."

"That's a great idea," Dallas said. "We could have an exhibition game. I know my Legion team would love to play."

"You could always play Gentry," Julie said dryly, remembering the fight at the Springfield tournament.

Dallas grinned at her. "Actually that's not a bad idea. Since the Gentry players are the same ones who play for the high school, that would point out that a smaller town has already formed a school team. So can we. Besides, Mel Cooney is both their coach and a Tribune teacher. I know he'd cooperate."

Dallas's hand slid from the back of the chair to Julie's shoulder and he patted her. She looked at him and they shared their little secret of the Gentry game.

"Hey, Julie, do you mind if I turn on the radio?" Norm asked. "We're broadcasting the Royals game. I just want to check the score." He pulled a tiny transistor radio from his shirt pocket and turned it on. It was already set to his station.

"You know you're in Royals country," Tennis said to Dallas. "It's only a couple hours drive to Kansas City. I've been to Cardinal games, but St. Louis is a few more hours away."

"I've seen the Royals play since I moved here. Are you going to a game while you're home?" Dallas asked.

"Wish I could. It's too late to get tickets. I guess I could get there early and go in general admission. I've done that before, but you're so far out, you can't even hear the crack of the bat."

Dallas pulled out his wallet, took out a card, and

studied it. "The Royals are in town tonight and this weekend. I might be able to get us some tickets if you're really interested. Say for tomorrow afternoon's game."

"You know somebody in KC?" Norm asked.

Dallas named a pitcher. "We were roommates on most of our road trips. He was traded last year."

"Hey, I'd love to go," Norm said.

"Me, too," Tennis chimed in.

"Julie?" Dallas said. His hand was still on her shoulder. "Would you like to fly up Saturday for a game?"

"Why not?" she said. She didn't want to upset the camaraderie of the group, but in her heart she dreaded another ball game.

"Do you mind if I use your phone?" he asked. At Julie's nod, he went inside, closing the patio door behind him.

In a very few minutes he was back.

"Okay, we're on. I got six tickets for Saturday's game. Two o'clock. I'll fly us up. How early do you want to be there?"

"How did you manage?" Tennis asked. "Isn't your friend at the game as we speak?"

"Yes. But he sent me a special phone number for the stadium. I spoke with his wife. We're to pick up the tickets at Gate C."

"Let's meet at the airport at ten," Norm suggested. "That'll give us plenty of time to take in the atmosphere, watch batting practice, and eat. This is great!"

"This is great!" Norm said as the group filed into their box seats between home plate and first.

The flight to KC had been pleasant, Julie had to admit.

Spirits were high. The enthusiasm of the group was limitless. Even she was looking forward to the game.

She wasn't prepared for the enormity of Royals Stadium. They were quite early, but they weren't the first ones there. The place buzzed with activity. After they had found their seats and established a home base, Dallas showed them around the stadium. Julie paid special attention to the bullpen, a place where Dallas had spent a great deal of time. She closed her eyes and pictured him in a uniform and wished she had seen him pitch. Maybe there were old videotapes of ball games. She'd have to ask her brothers. Their dedication to sports might finally come in handy.

They were seated, eating hot dogs, when a beautiful redhead came to their box.

"Dallas," she exclaimed and hugged him as soon as he stood.

Dallas introduced Kelli, his friend's wife. "J.J. wants to see you," she told him. "He's starting pitcher today. As soon as the game's over, you're to take your friends down to the south tunnel." She visited at length with Dallas, occasionally drawing Julie into their conversation. "Remember, the south tunnel," she said as she left.

"She seems nice," Julie commented.

"She's great," Dallas said. "It takes a special kind of woman to be married to a ballplayer who's gone half the time. She never complains about taking care of their kids by herself or dealing with household problems that would normally fall to the husband. J.J. knows he found a jewel in Kelli."

"Are you saying being a ballplayer isn't all glory?" Tennis asked.

"One motel room after another," he said. "That's one part I don't miss."

Tennis asked him question after question about his pro career. When Dallas went after another hot dog, Tennis turned to Julie.

"We're not dealing with a Bobby Lee here. You have to pry answers out of Dallas. He's not living on past glory. He's not hiding from his past, either. I like him."

"Me, too," Julie admitted.

Once the game started, Dallas explained each play to Julie, much as he had at the Springfield tournament. He called strikes before they came across the plate. He predicted the direction the Kansas City batters would hit. The opposing team was having its trouble at the plate.

In the fifth inning the score was three to nothing. Dallas was getting tense. He said less and less and anxiously watched each pitch.

"Do you realize that J.J. has a no—"

Dallas interrupted Tennis, "Don't say it. Don't mess it up."

"Don't say what?" Julie asked.

Tennis whispered in her ear. "No one has gotten on base by hitting the ball. Do you understand what I'm saying?"

Julie nodded. She had heard about no-hitters before because they were so rare. Her brother John had pitched one when he played Legion ball. He had bragged about it for years and still mentioned it on occasion.

At the end of the seventh inning, the score was four to nothing. Dallas was beside himself watching his friend's every windup. Every pitch. Julie found herself holding her breath as the tension built.

By the top of the ninth, Dallas wasn't moving. He had reached for Julie's hand as J.J. walked out to the mound. As each ball sailed toward the plate, he squeezed her hand. Then he would relax his hold, only to squeeze it tighter as the next pitch zoomed toward the batter.

*God, please help J.J.,* Julie prayed silently, then heard her petition aloud as Dallas's low voice murmured "Please help him, Lord."

The first batter hit a long fly to right field. It was easily caught. The second batter grounded to the second baseman and was thrown out at first.

The third batter stepped up to home plate. The first pitch was high and inside. He watched it go by. The second pitch was a strike. J.J. wound up and pitched. Ball two.

"Low and outside. Low and outside," Dallas chanted in a low voice. The next pitch was low and outside, but the batter swung. Strike two.

Julie was squeezing Dallas's hand.

"Two and two," Tennis said in a low voice.

Julie could hear Norm breathe behind her. The stands were silent, waiting.

J.J. let go of another low and outside. The batter was not fooled. Full count.

J.J. took off his hat and wiped the sweat from his brow with his sleeve. He shook his head no at the catcher. He shook it again. Then he nodded.

He wound up and pitched. The batter swung and fouled it off toward third base.

J.J. went through another silent discussion with the catcher.

"Low and outside. Low and outside," Dallas chanted.

J.J. threw another pitch. The batter swung and missed.

The crowd erupted, the noise was deafening. J.J. was surrounded by his teammates. Dallas hugged Julie enthusiastically, then drew away.

Julie sent a thank you heavenward, then looked over at Dallas who had his eyes shut momentarily. He opened them and gazed at Julie. A slow smile broke on his face and he squeezed her hand.

"Giving credit where credit's due," he said.

No one left the stadium. The standing ovation for J.J. continued. After five minutes, Dallas pulled Julie out into the aisle.

"Come on, we're going to the south tunnel." Tennis, Lisa, Carol, and Norm followed as they wound their way through the ecstatic fans.

Reporters swarmed the south tunnel. Julie spotted Kelli in the crush. Kelli saw them at the same time and pushed toward them. Dallas grabbed Kelli and hugged her.

"Stay close and follow me," he yelled at Julie. She hooked her finger through the belt loop on his slacks and hung on as they wove toward the daylight at the end of the tunnel. They came out onto the playing field.

J.J. was talking to a television reporter. He saw Kelli and ran for her, ignoring the reporter. He hugged her and when he saw Dallas, he hugged him too.

"I'm glad you're here, Dal. I could just hear you saying 'low and outside' over and over."

"You heard that?" Julie exclaimed.

J.J. laughed. "I heard that for years. Dallas mixed up pitches, but thought low and outside was the best in a clutch. And I was in a clutch situation when that last batter came up. Can you believe it, Kelli?" He hugged his wife again.

Dallas put his arm around Julie's shoulders. "This is Julie Russell," he said.

"Glad to meet you, J.J.," she said. "Congratulations!"

"J.J.," the TV reporter had followed him. "When did you know you had a no-hitter going?"

"After the first batter," he answered and grinned. "The pressure's always there. Every pitcher knows how many batters he's faced before one gets a hit."

"This is your first no-hitter. Did you have any idea the game would end like this?" the reporter asked.

"I was tense before the game, probably because Dallas was coming."

"Dallas Stone? Formerly with Chicago. I should have recognized you," the reporter said to Dallas. "I'm sure your fans would like to know where you are now and how's the back?"

"I'm fine and thrilled to be here to see J.J. pitch this record game. I almost stopped breathing when that last batter went a full count, then hit foul. J.J., how's the arm feeling now?" Dallas deftly shifted the subject from himself back to J.J.

"My arm feels great. Let's go on up to the booth." He walked toward the tunnel with his arm still around his wife. Dallas and Julie followed. The rest of their group had made it to the mouth of the tunnel and fell in behind Julie.

The crowd had begun to leave the stadium, so Julie's group made slow progress going against the flow. J.J. was hailed by all who saw him. Finally they were led into an elevator that whisked them to the press booth.

"I've always wanted to see what one of these was like," Norm said.

Across from the booth's view onto the field was a conference room where J.J. headed. He took a seat at a table loaded with microphones. Cameras were set up at the back of the room. The press, who had been in the booth across the hall, filed in and began asking questions. Julie leaned against the back wall, out of the way.

"My good friend Dallas Stone is here," J.J. said. "Come on up here, Dallas."

Dallas, standing beside Julie, shook his head slightly, but J.J. repeated that he wanted his friend beside him. Since the TV cameras were now pointed at him and not at J.J., Dallas made his way up the aisle to the table. This was J.J.'s moment. He didn't need to share it with him.

Julie watched him go forward, pride swelling her chest. Dallas was no Bobby Lee, just as Tennis had said. She saw his hesitation to join in J.J.'s limelight, and she admired him for it. She shook her head. She hated to admit it, but there was a lot she admired about the athlete Dallas Stone.

## nine

"I think it's a flattering picture," Tennis said. He sat in Julie's living room Monday morning studying the newspaper.

"They got my name wrong. Julia. I guess the reporter overheard Dallas introducing me to J.J. I don't know why they ran this picture instead of the one in the *Kansas City Star*. J.J. should have been the only one in the photo." She adjusted the sofa pillow behind her. "Would you like some more coffee?"

He shook his head. "Dallas Stone is news. He virtually dropped out of sight after the accident. With this AP picture, you're in papers across the country. That's pretty exciting stuff."

"A no-hitter is news, too."

"J.J. sure didn't mind sharing the spotlight."

"No, but Dallas minded," she said and was terribly proud of that fact. "I was surprised he agreed to schedule a news conference down here in exchange for no questions at J.J.'s press conference."

"He told me it would be good publicity for the committee. He might drum up some big supporters if it's written up right."

"But they might mix up the facts. Julia! I sound like an old maid schoolteacher."

"Well?" Tennis said then ducked as Julie threw a sofa pillow at him.

"I'm going to the drugstore to see if they still have some of yesterday's papers and if any of today's papers

99

ran this picture. Coming?" Tennis asked.

"No. Wouldn't that seem just a bit on the vain side?"

"No, *Julia*. Just research for the committee. I'm telling you this publicity can translate into big bucks for them. They might actually get that team." Tennis stood and folded the paper so that Julie's picture showed.

"Tennis, you sound as if you don't want them to get it."

"I think the same way you do. We have too many sports in education. I've always enjoyed the major leagues, but I don't think high schools need to be their farm clubs."

"But you went to that committee meeting," she argued.

"I wanted to see Dallas in action. After all, my best friend is interested in him. And I like the guy. He seems well rounded. I've not made a public stand against the committee. I'm just telling you. Come on, let's go get those other papers."

Reluctantly Julie went with him. There wasn't a large assortment of newspapers at the drugstore, but Tennis bought one of each.

"Let's go somewhere and look through them," he said and ushered her back to the car. Julie thought he meant back at her duplex or over a cup of coffee at a cafe, but he drove them straight to The Sports World.

"Well, Dallas, you're a celebrity," he said as soon as they were settled in Dallas's glass office.

"Looks like it. Julia, this is a good picture of you," he said.

"Can you believe they did that? My fifteen minutes of fame and my name's not even right."

Dallas laughed. "You'll find you can't believe everything you read in the papers, and I'm not just talking about the tabloids. After a while you develop a tough skin. It comes with the territory."

Tennis handed out the papers and opened one to the sports page. "Here you are," he said. "St. Louis ran the one of the four of you. Kelli took a good picture, too. And they got her name right."

"They have it on record," Dallas said.

"Springfield has us," Julie said, folding up her paper.

"They should have run the one just of J.J.," Dallas said. "Throwing a no-hitter is a once in a lifetime thrill."

"Didn't you throw two?" Tennis asked.

"I was blessed."

"We were fortunate to get to see that game yesterday," Tennis said. "Thanks again, Dallas."

"I enjoyed it, too," Julie said and meant it. She was as surprised as the others looked, but it had been fun and definitely exciting.

"We may convert you after all. Looks like all the local papers ran your picture, Julia," Dallas said.

Julie made a face at him.

"I've already been called about the press conference. The reporters will be here on Thursday. We're going to do the interview right here in the store. Might be good for business. We put a rush on the baseball caps."

Dallas's picture and interview were printed around the country.

"Listen to this," Julie said Friday morning, reading the article to Tennis as if he hadn't already seen it. "Donations can be sent to the baseball committee in care of

Stone's sporting goods store, The Sports World, in Tribune, Missouri. This sure puts us on the map." She laid the paper on her coffee table.

"The money will pour in now," Tennis said sarcastically.

"Tennis, don't you feel a bit hypocritical? You're against the committee raising funds, and yet you act like Dallas is your good friend."

"Me hypocritical? What about you? You don't think we need this ball team anymore than I do. Yet, you're dating the guy."

"He knows how I feel about adding a baseball team. I've been straight with him from the beginning."

"Let's not argue on my last day in Tribune. Come on. I'm taking you to lunch. I'm leaving at the crack of dawn tomorrow and have yet to pack and draw a route on the map. Let's get moving."

Lunch was a bittersweet affair for Julie. She knew she wouldn't see Tennis again for some time.

"Will you be back for Christmas?" she asked when he took her back to her duplex.

"I plan on it. We get a long break. And I want to see you, Julie."

"Of course you want to see me," Julie said, puzzled by his tone.

Tennis took her in his arms. She thought he was just going to hug her, but he kissed her full on the lips instead.

"Tennis?" she asked, bewildered by what had just happened.

"Julie, I've been thinking—we're so alike. Maybe when I get back at Christmas we could see if anything

develops between us." He still held her and not in a "just
friends" manner. Julie stepped back.

"Tennis, what's going on here? We're friends."

"I know, but couldn't our friendship develop into a
serious relationship?"

"I don't know what to say." She closed her eyes and
asked for God's guidance. She didn't want to say the
wrong thing and hurt her dearest friend.

"I love you, Tennis. You are the best friend I've ever
had." She paused, thinking of how to phrase her words.

"It's Dallas, isn't it?"

Julie looked Tennis straight in the eyes and nodded.

"I guess that's what this is all about. I see you slipping
away. Dallas is taking my place. And I don't want to lose
you."

Julie gave him a big bear hug.

"You silly man. You can't lose me, no matter how
hard you try. I do care about Dallas. He's very special to
me, but not in the same way that you are."

"I know. Sorry I brought this up. Ego, I guess. You
know, I like Dallas."

"I know."

"Well, I'd better shove off. I've got a million things to
do before tomorrow."

"Okay." Julie kissed him on the cheek. "Now drive
carefully on your trip and I'll keep you in my prayers."

She hugged him hard.

"See you at Christmas," he said and winked as he
opened the door.

That afternoon Julie moped around her duplex. She
was still bothered by Tennis's overture, which had
caught her totally off guard. She thought they had

cleared the air before he left. She would write him a chatty letter that afternoon, so he would have mail soon after he arrived at his new home.

That action brought her peace about Tennis, but what about his words concerning Dallas and the committee? She didn't want to think about them together. Weren't they two separate entities? Did not supporting one mean not supporting the other?

"God, please help me decide. I can't hurt him," she prayed out loud.

How much easier it would have been if she had fallen in love with Tennis. They had so much in common. They thought alike, they had similar goals. They had been friends for so long, but that special spark was missing.

That special spark, that magic attraction was there with Dallas. Oh, no! That didn't mean she was in love with him, did it? Love an athlete? It didn't bear thinking about. Yet she could think of nothing else.

Around four, the object of her thoughts called.

"How about a movie tonight?" Dallas asked.

"I'd like that," Julie answered.

"I would have asked you earlier, but I thought you would be seeing Tennis on his last night here. I ran into him downtown and he told me he had had lunch with you and already said goodbye."

That night Dallas repeated that he would have asked her earlier if he had known she was free.

"It was considerate of you to think that I would like to spend time with Tennis."

"Oh, I'm not so considerate," Dallas said. "As a matter of fact, I didn't like Tennis at first. I thought he was competition."

"I can see how you would think that. We've been best friends forever, but never involved in a romantic sense." *Nor will we ever be,* she added silently. Being with Dallas reinforced the difference in her feelings toward the two men.

"While I'm at it," Dallas continued, "I might as well confess."

"Confess?"

"I didn't know who Harold Pinter was. I had to look him up in the library. I know now. I read a biography and several of his plays. Then Tennis didn't mention him again, and I sure wasn't going to." Dallas felt a weight lift off his shoulders now that he'd told her the truth.

Julie laughed. "You went to all that trouble for me? I'm flattered."

"Good. Then it was worth it," he said and pushed his hand through his hair. He wanted Julie to know him and know him well. "Since I'm being so honest—I don't care for classical music."

"Classical music? Oh...," she said as she remembered the symphony she'd asked him to attend in Joplin. "Have you ever been to the symphony?"

"Never."

"Then you must reserve your opinion until you've heard a live performance. Besides, I already have the tickets. And, if you want, we can go early enough to have dinner at one of Joplin's Chinese restaurants."

"Now that is a draw." Dallas pointed to the marquee. "What about tonight? We have our choice of two movies."

They agreed on a movie and stood in line.

"Dallas," Lon Feldman, the committee treasurer,

stepped up to their place in line. "You won't believe the pledges that have come in today. People have called me at home."

"I've had a few calls myself," Dallas said. "We'll see if the checks come in the mail next week."

"That article was a stroke of brilliance. I'll bet we've got five thousand dollars and we haven't even started."

"That's good, because we're going to need a lot more than five thousand to get this program going. Two, please," he said at the ticket window.

Lon Feldman walked them to the ticket taker and continued to talk. They were joined by a couple of other men who were on the baseball committee. It sounded as if they had memorized the article about Dallas.

"Go on in. I'll be there in a minute," Lon told his wife. The other men waved their dates and wives on, too.

Julie leaned against the wall and waited for the conversation to end. Baseball, baseball, baseball. It never ended.

She listened to the animated conversation. The men looked up to Dallas in more than one way, she observed. He towered over all of them. And he was a leader. She might go to the next committee meeting just to see him in action. Then she would work hard at separating in her mind the committee from the man.

The crowd pouring into the theater dwindled. Only a few remained at the popcorn counter. Julie walked over and looked at the candy selection. She checked out the video machines that dotted the lobby. Still the men talked on.

Finally, Lon's wife came toward them.

"You've missed the first ten minutes," she said.

"Come on. I'll fill you in."

Dallas looked at Julie as the group dispersed. "Sorry. I had no idea they'd be so long-winded. Do you want to go on in or do something else?"

"Let's get some popcorn and leave. Maybe you can cash in the tickets and we can come another night. In a mystery like this, it's hard to pick up the plot if you don't see it all."

"I'm really sorry," Dallas said again after he had returned the tickets for a refund. He opened the car door for her. "Shall we try it again tomorrow night?"

"Sure."

Dallas drove them around town while they ate the popcorn. They toured the square like the teenagers. He drove by his sister's house. Lights were on, but there were no extra cars in the driveway.

"Do you mind if we stop in and see my sister."

"Should we call first?"

"Not since we're already here. Marti and Hal are family. They'll tell me if it's inconvenient."

Marti seemed glad to see them. "Hal's in the shower. He just finished mowing the yard. How about a glass of lemonade?" She led them toward the kitchen.

"No big party tonight? What's wrong?" Dallas asked.

"We're going out tomorrow night. We thought it would be nice to stay in tonight. Get the weekend chores done early."

"What you need are a couple of kids," Dallas said. "That would keep you home with a purpose."

"Dallas, you sound like a hopeful grandmother," Julie said.

"Thank you, Julie," Marti said. "He's always on my

case about kids. Have some of your own, Dallas."

"I plan on it—someday." He looked at Julie and cocked an eyebrow. Julie felt a blush rising.

Hal joined them in the kitchen and fixed himself a big glass of lemonade. "You all want to play Scrabble? We haven't played in a long time, Dal."

"Okay, Julie?"

"Fine." She took a seat at the kitchen table. Marti brought out the Scrabble set, and Julie helped turn over the tiles.

Julie won the game, but with only eight points higher than Dallas's score.

He had surprised her. He even knew one word that she'd never heard of, and when she had challenged him, he'd dug out the dictionary and proved it was a word.

Conversation with his sister and brother-in-law flowed smoothly. Of course the committee came up. Dallas told Hal about the phone calls promising money. "We'll see how much comes in."

It all came in, plus more. By the end of the week, the committee treasury balance was over ten thousand dollars, and most of it was from donations outside of town. People had read the article and sent money. The sentiment seemed to be that Dallas Stone had suffered enough. He at least deserved to have a ball team in the high school to keep him in the game.


"That newspaper article failed to mention that I coached a Legion team," Dallas told Julie on their flight to Joplin on Friday night. "I sure don't want pity from people."

"I think it's more concern," Julie said. She had been

watching the Missouri landscape below the plane, but at his words, she turned to gaze at Dallas's profile. "They genuinely like you. Ten thousand dollars is a lot of money."

"It isn't nearly enough. We project that will pay for the first year. The second and third years won't cost as much—maybe seven thousand apiece."

"You'll get there," Julie encouraged him, and then she wondered why she had. She was still against adding baseball to the sports curriculum.

Her brother Tom and his girlfriend, Elaine, picked them up at the airport, and the four of them dined at Grand Fortuna.

"The atmosphere alone beats Tribune's Chinese place," Julie said.

"Yes, but do they have good fortune cookies? That's the test," Tom joked. "Will the fortune mean something?"

"The current year will bring you happiness," Julie read hers at the end of the meal. She looked up to see Dallas smiling at her and she smiled back.

"A full moon will bring travel," Dallas read.

"That's true. There's a full moon tonight and we're flying back to Tribune," Julie said.

"I was hoping for a bigger trip," Dallas said. "I may go home over Labor Day. Of course, there won't be a full moon in another week."

"You're going to see your Mom?"

"Yes. I think Marti and Hal will go with me. There's an annual family reunion each September."

"That sounds like fun. Speaking of family, would you like to go to Sunday dinner again this weekend?" Julie had been seeing Dallas each night since the Saturday before. Teachers' workshops had started on Wednesday. Sunday was her last day before school started.

"Sure," he answered. "Will you be there, Tom?"

"No. The semester's already started. I need to start hitting the books." He glanced at Elaine. Julie knew he wouldn't be studying alone.

"I think we should go," Julie said. "Hearing the instruments tune up is the same as watching batting practice before a game."

Dallas raised his eyebrows at that and she laughed. "You're going to love it. You'll see."

"It really is something," Tom said. "Julie made me go the first time. Now I wouldn't miss it."

"I thought you said your brothers only think of sports and don't pay attention to you," Dallas whispered to her as they rode in the back seat of Tom's car. "Sounds to me like you influenced Tom's taste in music."

Julie looked thoughtful.

When they arrived at the performing arts center, the lobby was already crowded. "Let's find our seats," Julie said. "I can hardly wait."

They sat in the balcony and watched as the concertmaster played an A and the musicians tuned their instruments.

The first piece was a Rossini overture. Dallas actually enjoyed the music. The theme was stated by a quartet of horns and repeated several times throughout the overture. He liked the brass section.

"Oh, no. Ives," Julie said as applause died down.

"Someone you know?"

"No." She held up her program. "The American composer Ives. His sound is rather discordant. His music isn't what I would have chosen for your first time at the symphony. There are even two rhythms going on at one time. And remember, don't applaud between movements. That's quite gauche."

She was right on target, Dallas decided. Ives was not his idea of music. It was more like instruments warming up for a rap session where everyone played a different tune. How the man beside him could snore through it was beyond him.

"A critic," he said to Julie and motioned toward the sleeping man.

She laughed. That was a sound Dallas loved.

At intermission they strolled outside to get some fresh air, although it was much warmer outside on the late August evening.

"You're going to like Beethoven," Julie told him. "His eighth symphony is fun."

Fun? Dallas questioned that as they took their seats back in the air conditioned hall.

"You were right," he told her afterward as they flew toward Tribune. "Beethoven was wonderful. Such a difference between him and Ives. Why would they play that other stuff?"

"There are some redeeming qualities to his work. His compositions are very intricate and appeal to some people."

"I don't see how. I read in the program notes that Ives had to sell insurance on the side. I can see why. There's no way he could have made a living writing sounds like that."

Julie laughed. "There are many aspects to his work."

She thought for a moment of how to make him understand. "Okay. Take Pete Rose. Some baseball fans don't like the way he acted on and off the field as an all-around athlete, but they like the techniques he used to get hit after hit. Am I making any sense?"

"Maybe," Dallas admitted.

"Well, other than Ives, did you enjoy the symphony?"

"Yes," he said emphatically. "The only other live orchestra I've heard was in high school and it was pitiful. When the musicians are this gifted, it's entirely different. Thanks for making me come."

"I didn't make you."

"Yes, you did. Just by asking, you made me. I wanted to compromise. You've gone with me to ball games and now I've gone with you to a symphony. A trade off, see?"

"Yes, I do."

"It should be the same way with your family. Maybe you need to start the compromising."

"I'm trying," Julie answered. "I've talked to God about it and I'm really trying to work through my attitude about sports."

"That's all I can ask," Dallas said.

That evening when he stood on her doorstep, he kissed her good night. It was different from the little kisses he had given her from time to time. It was special to Julie, just like the evening had been.


Sunday they attended early service together and again Dallas helped Julie with her class. Taking the lesson from Romans 12, the two encouraged the students to discover and use the special gifts God had given them.

"You're very good with children," Julie told him as they drove toward her folks' home.

"I like kids," he said. "I like pointing them in the right direction."

Before Sunday dinner, while Julie and Evelyn were in the kitchen, Dallas wandered over to the trophy case. He had been praying about how to help the Russells show Julie that she was as important to them as the athletes in the family.

"Charles," he called to Julie's father. "Does it bother you that one of your children is left out of this showcase?"

Charles ambled to the end of the living room.

"You're talking about Julie."

"Yes," Dallas answered. It was time to get the issue out in the open, and he hoped he could do it without alienating Charles.

"I can hardly put a bunch of papers in a trophy case." He opened the door of an antique cabinet and pulled out a large scrapbook. "Here's where we keep Julie's stuff."

Charles carried the book to the couch and motioned for Dallas to sit down.

"This here's when Julie won an essay contest." He pointed to a newspaper article and a certificate. "She was in third grade. She's always had brains," he said proudly.

"Does Julie know this?"

"Sure. We've got everything she's done in here."

"Julie," Dallas called toward the kitchen. "Come here."

Julie appeared in the doorway. Dallas patted the couch beside him.

"What?" she asked, but sat down beside him. "Oh, Dad, are you boring Dallas with the scrapbook of my childhood?"

Evelyn walked into the living room and smiled at the scene. "He might be more interested in volume two or three."

"Volume two?" Julie echoed.

"Sure, that one ends when you were about fifteen." She walked over to the cabinet. "Julie's accomplished a lot in her life," she boasted to Dallas as she lifted two other large books and carried them to him.

"You kept this up?" Julie asked in amazement.

"Of course, honey," Evelyn said.

Dallas opened the book and thumbed through it until he found a program from Julie's Phi Theta Kappa initiation. He nudged Julie and pointed to it.

"You didn't even come to this," Julie said.

"We couldn't, Julie. We were too busy here. We had two calves that night and almost lost one of the mothers. Remember that night, Charles?"

He nodded. "I ruined my good shoes. We were all dressed to leave when everything happened at once. Didn't have time to change clothes until bedtime."

"I thought you didn't want to come," Julie said.

"Where'd you get a silly notion like that?" Evelyn asked. "I had to write to the college to get the program."

Julie shrugged, unable to speak.

"Do Julie and I have time for a walk to the creek before lunch?" Dallas asked.

Evelyn considered her watch. "About half an hour. The others will be here by then."

"Plenty of time," he said. He pulled Julie to her feet

and led her outside.

They walked together, his arm around her shoulders, supporting her, her arm around his waist. Julie's tears ran down her cheeks. When they stopped beside the creek, Dallas pulled her into his arms and held her while she sobbed quietly into his shirt. When she calmed down, he dug a handkerchief from his pocket and handed it to her.

"I think God just showed you that your special gifts are appreciated," Dallas said.

# ten

The first day of school was as much an ordeal for the teachers as for the students. Julie appeared stern and in control as she met each new class, but inwardly she was as keyed up as the students.

Crowded lunch periods, lockers that wouldn't open, lost students, late buses, and names she couldn't begin to pronounce left her exhausted at the end of the day, but by the grace of God she'd gotten through it.

Once home, she flung herself face down onto the couch, working her shoes off and letting them fall where they would. She barely had the strength to answer the phone when it rang. As it was, she had let it ring seven times before she answered. She was not surprised to hear Dallas's voice.

"I was hoping we could have dinner together. Celebrate the first day of school."

"If this house were on fire, I'd still not leave," she said.

"That bad a day?"

"Typical first day of school. It must have been a hundred and five in my room. By seventh period, the smell of twenty-five sweating adolescents was nauseating."

"Sounds like a baseball locker room. But you still need to eat. Why don't I bring dinner over?"

"All right. But, I may still be lying on the couch when you get here."

"Was that twenty-five sweaty adolescents and one

116

sweaty teacher?"

"Okay, okay. I'll take a shower. See you later."

She stood under the shower for a long time, the soothing spray revitalizing her. She decided on shorts and a short-sleeved top for the evening.

Julie was sitting at the kitchen table going over her class lists when Dallas knocked.

"Come in," she called toward the door.

Dallas strode in carrying a pizza. "Pepperoni," he announced.

"Smells wonderful. Coke?"

"I'll get it. Stay seated. What are you doing? Grading homework already?"

"No. These are preliminary class lists. I won't put them in my grade book until next week when all last minute changes are made."

"May I see them?" he asked and handed her a drink.

"Sure." Julie grabbed a napkin and placed one on the table for Dallas. He sat down and reached for her hand, as was his habit when they ate together.

"Thank you, Lord, for this food and the blessings You have given us this day. Amen," Dallas offered grace.

"Amen," Julie said and tackled a piece of pizza. "Mmmm. Extra cheese?"

"My favorite." He studied Julie's class lists before reaching for a piece. "You have some of my Legion ball– players in this sixth period class."

"I recognized some of the players' names from your party. I knew a lot of them would be juniors this year. I'm trying to get names in my mind. I teach six classes and have a planning period. That's 162 names to learn."

"That many. What's your method?"

"I'm one of those teachers you probably hated. I seat them alphabetically until I can learn their names. By about the third week, I'll let them sit where they want, but I'll still use a seating chart. It's a lot more effective to use their names when I call on them. Makes them want to be better prepared. At least, that's my assumption."

Dallas flipped through the sheets. "Five classes of English and one of English literature. Cleve Owens is in the lit class. He's a good infielder."

"Yes, I remember seeing him at your party. He's a senior and a good student. He was in my junior English class last year."

"You have Brad Williams in English. He's one of my pitchers. You have your own nephew in class?"

"Yes. Jimmie's in junior English. I'm the only one who teaches it and it's required. Remember I had Brad in the summer when I taught sophomore English. He barely got a C. He'll have to work hard this year. And so will I. I'm also the faculty sponsor of the school newspaper." She put down her piece of pizza, walked over to a stack of newspapers on the end table, and brought one back to Dallas.

"We put out one a month. Nine issues. The first one comes out tomorrow. Last year's group worked on it. All I did was check the dates of the club meetings and insert the football schedule. I found last year that we couldn't get an issue out quickly enough with all the information the students needed—map of the school, that sort of thing. At the end of the year, we'll get next fall's paper ready. I'll show you."

"Hey, this is pretty slick."

"Thanks. Getting it out early stirs up interest in the paper's staff. Our first staff meeting is Wednesday after school. This pizza's great," Julie added and reached for another piece.

"Do you have any other extra duties?"

"I'm junior class sponsor. That means a float for football homecoming and decorations for the prom. At least those projects are at different times of the year."

"Do you attend the prom?"

"Oh, yes. I'm a chaperone."

"I'll take you," he offered.

"It's a long way off."

"I plan on being around. It'll be fun going back to high school again. What color dress will you wear so I can get a corsage."

Julie laughed. "I'll let you know. I might spring for a new one." She lifted one hand daintily. "I simply can't appear two years running in the same dress. It just isn't done."

"It's black tie these days, isn't it?"

"Yes. And a fancy dinner before the dance. Some students even rent limousines from Joplin. It's way out of hand. Sure you want to go?"

"I'm sure. I might skip the limo, though." He turned the page of the school newspaper. "I'm impressed. This looks professional."

"The *Tribune Daily News* prints it for us. I'm rather proud of it."

"Could you do an article on the baseball committee?"

"I don't know," Julie said and hesitated. "I don't know if we can promote something like that. I'll have to ask the administration."

"Censorship?"

"Not exactly. Dallas, I'm not sure where I stand on this issue. I know it means a lot to you, but I still feel that we are sports heavy. What we need are more library books and more literacy programs."

"I see. I thought you'd changed your mind. You've always been encouraging."

"I don't know what I feel anymore," Julie said truthfully. She wanted Dallas to succeed, but that contradicted her stand on no more sports at the high school. "I really don't know," she repeated.

Dallas locked gazes with her. "I thought you were beginning to understand."

"I don't know," she said again. "But I will check about the committee. It's news. As long as we present an unbiased picture, I'm sure it will be okay."

"I can give you hard facts in a couple of weeks. We have another meeting tomorrow night to map our campaign. I'll be giving lots of talks before groups, trying to raise funds."

"All right. Dallas," she said and paused, trying to find the right words. "I'll keep an open mind." And she vowed that she would.

He smiled at her. "That's all I can ask."

Dallas frowned to himself as he realized that Julie still wasn't sure about baseball. For him it was part of life. Not all consuming, but important. She needed more time, he decided. Time to know him better. And she would get it.

"Julie, over Labor Day, Marti, Hal, and I are flying home to see my family. We'll leave early Saturday morning and come back sometime Monday. Would you go with me?"

Julie swallowed her bite of pizza and looked Dallas straight in the eyes. "Yes. I'd love to meet your family," she said simply.

The first week of school whizzed by with a minimum of schedule changes and interruptions. Julie rose early each morning and worked late each evening, grading papers and finalizing lesson plans for the following week so she would have nothing to do over the Labor Day weekend except enjoy her visit to Kentucky. She asked Cindy to teach her Sunday school class so her calendar would be free. With a light heart, she packed her suitcase Friday night.

By eight o'clock Saturday morning, Dallas had finished the pre-flight check of the plane. Marti and Julie sat in the back seat while Hal sat in the co-pilot's seat.

"Perfect weather for flying," Marti said as they taxied down the runway. "Do you mind a small plane?"

"Not anymore," Julie answered in a loud voice so she could be heard over the engine noise. "I have great confidence in Dallas, but I still say a little prayer for our safety before we take off." She looked down as the plane lifted into the sky. The town dropped below them and soon they were flying over checkerboard fields.

"How long a trip is it?" she asked Marti.

"About three hours. Want something to drink? We've got a cooler of pop to ward off any air sickness."

"I'm fine, thanks." The engine noise discouraged conversation, so Julie leaned back in her seat and watched out the window, her mind running over what she knew of Dallas's family and what she might expect of the weekend.

He'd said little about his sister who lived in Owensboro, only mentioning once that she was married and had two children. He'd talked more about his mother, but Julie still didn't have a clear picture of her. She knew Mrs. Stone had to be a strong woman to have worked through the trauma of her husband's death and gone on with her life.

Julie leaned up toward Dallas and touched his arm to get his attention.

"Are we there yet?" she asked.

Dallas grinned playfully at her. "Almost," he said and turned back to the instruments in front of him. "We've got a good wind, so we're ahead of schedule."

Before eleven o'clock, Dallas made his final approach to the Owensboro airport and slipped the plane onto the runway in a smooth landing. Dallas climbed out and helped his passengers, then he and Hal unloaded the luggage.

"Mom," Marti shouted and ran with her arms outstretched toward a woman who walked briskly toward the plane.

Julie watched the two women embrace. Marti was several inches taller than her mother, whom Julie guessed to be more her own petite height. Dallas reached the twosome and hugged his mother and then led her toward Julie.

"Mom, this is Julie Russell."

"Dallas has told me so much about you, Julie. I'm so glad you could come with him for the reunion."

"I'm delighted he asked me, Mrs. Stone."

"None of that Mrs. Stone business. That's my

mother-in-law's name. I'm Nellie."

"Okay, Nellie," Julie said and thought that the name fit Dallas's mother. Her bright blue eyes sparkled with life and she wore her brown hair, which was liberally sprinkled with gray, stylishly short. Julie reached for her bag, but Dallas picked it up and carried it with his.

"I figured Karen would be sent to get us," Dallas told his mother as they walked to her car.

"She wanted to, but she's got her hands full today. Little Jason has a cold and wants his mama with him every minute. They'll be over at the house later this afternoon. Some of the others arrived yesterday. Julie, you're going to be meeting more of our relatives than you can keep straight."

"She put me through that with her family," Dallas said. "It's her time to sort out names and faces." He stashed the suitcases in the trunk and then went into the airport terminal to make arrangements for his plane.

"Is Aunt Daisy here?" Marti asked.

"Arrived yesterday at noon," Nellie said. "Now she's Dallas's favorite," she told Julie. "You'll have to get her talking about Dallas as a little boy. She remembers every little scrap he ever got into, things I tend to push out of my mind."

Julie laughed. This could be a fun reunion. That thought stayed with her even after they arrived at the Stone home and she met the first wave of relatives.

"How many more are you expecting? And where are you going to put them all?" Julie asked Nellie.

"Some are staying over at Karen's house. I have a sister who lives here, and she's putting up a few, too. The kids always stretch out on the floor with sleeping bags. We make do. I'll show you your room, such as it is."

Julie learned she was in with Marti and her cousins Susan and Louise. Nellie had borrowed cots and rollaways from friends and neighbors and set up wards in the family room and in the larger bedrooms.

Great Aunt Daisy turned out to be a live wire. She had celebrated her eighty-fourth birthday only days before and was proud of it. She still lived alone and mowed her own yard, she told Julie. Then she launched into a recital of Dallas's finer points.

"He's one of the nicest boys I know," she told Julie, who smiled at Aunt Daisy calling Dallas a "boy." "He's gone through some tough times and come out smiling. He's a fighter and a winner. And he sure has found a good match in you."

"Why, thanks, Aunt Daisy," Julie said, wondering how exactly she was to respond to that. The older woman had assumed that she was a special person to Dallas, and she found herself hoping the same thing.

Lunch was a circus. The group numbered twenty-three, and all gathered in the large dining room to hold hands around the table while Nellie Stone's brother James said grace. That was the only quiet moment. The din grew deafening as the relatives filled their plates with the Colonel's finest chicken and found places to sit all over the house. Dallas and Julie ended up sitting in the swing on the front porch.

"How are you doing?" he asked. "Holding your own?"

"This is wonderful," Julie said. "Just like a family should be. Reminds me of my family, but on a grander scale."

They hadn't finished lunch when Karen and her family arrived. Dallas's older sister kissed him hello and handed him a little boy who immediately started crying for his mother.

"He's not feeling well. Sorry. He's usually a happy little guy," she explained and took the crying two-year-old from Dallas and hugged him to her chest.

"Hi, Uncle Dallas." A little girl climbed into the swing between Dallas and Julie and gave him a big hug.

"Hi, Ginger," Dallas said and grinned. "You want some chicken?"

Ginger lifted a drumstick off Dallas's plate and took a big bite.

"I guess she does," he said.

Julie had watched Karen as she carried Jason inside the house and back out again. Karen looked tired, and Julie recognized the worn-out look of motherhood that sometimes descended on her sister and sisters-in-law.

"Excuse me," she said to Dallas. She took her plate into the kitchen and then found Karen.

"Would you let me hold him awhile? He'll probably just cry for a moment, but then he'll be all right."

Karen gladly handed her son to Julie. As Julie expected, he started whimpering, but she walked with him away from his mother and out the back door, crooning softly to him the entire time.

Dallas found her sitting in the backyard under a shade tree, holding the sleeping child. He knelt down beside her.

"Karen told me you had Jason out here," he whispered. "Want me to take him?"

Julie shook her head. "We're fine. Go visit with your

relatives. We'll come in when he wakes up," she whispered.

Dallas leaned over and kissed Julie on the cheek. "Thanks. You're one in a million."

Basking in the glow of his praise, Julie sat contentedly holding the little boy. It was almost an hour later that Jason awoke. He looked at Julie and sat up.

"Mama?" he said.

"Let's go find her," Julie answered.

She carried him toward the house and was met by Karen, who admitted she'd been checking out the window every few minutes to make sure Jason was all right.

"Actually, I was checking to make sure you were okay. He's a heavy load."

"Oh, I'm fine," Julie said, although one arm was still asleep.

Dallas joined them and nonchalantly slipped his arm around Julie's shoulders. "I want you to meet the new arrivals," he said. "Buck just got here," he told his sister.

"And I'll bet you're bunking with him," Karen said and laughed.

"Yep. Can't break up the dynamic duo."

"Do I detect a history of mischief here?" Julie asked.

Dallas didn't answer, but led her to a huge man, at least six–feet–six and three hundred pounds. Dallas introduced them.

"Buck and I went all through high school together," Dallas said.

"We were great on the football team. I blocked so he could score. And boy did he score. With the ladies as well as touchdowns. And I see you've scored again," Buck said with a wink at Julie. "He always gets the pretty ones."

"I think I'd like to have a private conversation with Buck," Julie said.

"Not on your life," Dallas said and laughed. "Besides, he makes up half of what he says. I was a perfect little angel in school."

Buck guffawed, a deep infectious sound, attracting the attention of the others. Three more cousins joined Buck and Dallas and Julie, and they moved out to the front porch to relive old times. Each one had a bigger story to tell about Dallas. He kept a possessive arm on Julie and denied each tale or at least portions of it.

"Why are you all doing this to me?" he asked. "Julie thinks I'm a nice guy."

"It's our duty to tell her about the real Dallas Stone," his cousins teased. "Be criminal not to tell her."

The light-hearted atmosphere filled the evening. A few of the younger set took in a movie, but Dallas and Julie stayed at the Stone house and visited.

Although she went to bed before midnight, it was after two before Julie got to sleep. Marti, Susan, and Louise kept her awake whispering after all the lights were out. It reminded Julie of a high school slumber party and the subject was the same. Boys, or rather, men. She learned all about Susan's husband and Hal and the man Louise was dating who wasn't at the reunion. The cousins also told her about Dallas, and this time there was no need for Dallas to defend himself. Everything they said was positive.

"Whenever he played ball in Cleveland, he always sent us tickets," Susan said. "The best seats in the house. He'd introduce us to the players afterward. He's the most generous man. Kind, thoughtful, sincere—"

"You don't have to sell me on him," Julie interrupted. "I'm already convinced."

"He went through a hard time when he had to quit baseball," Marti offered."

"I know. He told me about it," Julie said.

"He did? He doesn't mention it to just anybody," Marti said. "I think I detect a real romance here."

"We'll see," Julie said noncommittally and rolled over and pretended she was trying to sleep. What did she feel toward Dallas? Admiration? Certainly. Respect? Yes. Love? She hesitated over the word, but finally admitted that she loved Dallas Stone, an athlete, and loved him with all her heart. But what should she do about it? How did he feel? She fell asleep without any answers.

The next morning the entire clan descended on the church Dallas had attended most of his life. Julie sat beside Dallas and her heart flipped when he reached for her hand and held it during the service.

*I'm acting like a high school girl,* she told herself, yet the special feeling continued throughout the morning. She listened to the sermon on tolerance of others' opinions and shared a significant look with Dallas. *Perhaps we could both be a little more tolerant of each others' beliefs on sports,* Julie thought.

It looked as if Dallas were thinking the same thing.

## eleven

The flight back to Tribune was uneventful. Life returned to normal, or almost normal. Julie was immersed in school activities. Dallas was enveloped by the baseball committee.

As soon as the committee met to finalize their budget and their campaign, Dallas was committed to night meetings. Each time before he met with a group, he took out his Bible and read Isaiah 41:10.

"So do not fear, for I am with you; do not be dismayed, for I am your God. I will strengthen you and help you; I will uphold you with my righteous right hand" (NIV).

The words gave him the courage to face the many civic groups in town. He spoke at Kiwanis, Rotary, Lions, the Downtown Association, the Chamber of Commerce, and the Association of University Women. The latter was the toughest group he faced. Julie was a member.

He hadn't realized she would be at the Saturday morning meeting, and it made him nervous to stare out at the crowd and see her. She sat at the side of the room, and after the first few minutes, he made sure he didn't look anywhere near her.

"Many of you are mothers and have sons who are in the Little League program." His voice sounded tinny to him. He cleared his throat, thought of Isaiah 41:10, and went on.

"When they get older, they can continue to play if the American Legion continues to sponsor a team. If not, they'll have nowhere to play, unless we get a team in the high school."

"But won't that be for only a few players? The best ones?" a woman asked.

"That's true. There will be training sessions and try-outs. The team would have fifteen to eighteen members. Those who didn't make the cut could serve as trainers, scorekeepers, in support positions."

"Would there be a grade average requirement?" another woman asked.

"Yes. Currently Tribune High School requires its athletes to maintain a C average. However, statistics gathered from surrounding high schools with baseball teams show that the team average is way above that. In fact, there are some teams that have a B+ average. Ballplayers spend a lot of time practicing and keeping in shape. They must be organized to keep a balance between school work and baseball."

Dallas had foreseen that question and had called coaches in the area to obtain his statistics.

"Which is more important? School work or baseball?" a woman asked in a belligerent voice.

"School work, of course. At the same time, a ballplayer has a responsibility to the team to be at a game and play his best, even if he has a test the next day. That brings up the organization I mentioned before. Baseball players have to plan ahead. They can't count on cramming the night before a test or finishing a paper the day before it's due."

Julie raised her hand and Dallas was forced to look in her direction.

"Yes, Julie," he said, knowing he was announcing to

the membership that he knew her. He had merely nodded at the other women, giving them permission to ask their questions.

"Could the committee raise enough money to pay for a tutor, in case some of the boys needed extra help. Won't they be missing some classes on days they have afternoon baseball games in other towns?"

"Yes. Many ball games are played in the afternoon and evening. Double–headers eliminate the extra expense of traveling to the same town to play again later in the season. The team would play the other towns in our football and basketball conference."

"Do they all have ball teams?" Julie asked.

"All but two of them do. Julie, I think your suggestion of a tutor is a valid one, and I'll present it to the committee."

"He's cute as can be," a woman at her table whispered to Julie. Julie looked down at her lap, hoping no one else had heard that comment directed at her.

"Are there any other questions?" Dallas asked. He pointed to a woman at a back table.

"What about sportsmanship?"

He was tempted to say "what about it?" and force her to restate her question. He couldn't tell if she was for the formation of a team or against it.

"Sportsmanship is a quality directed by the coach and the parents. Winning is important. But it isn't everything. If a player throws a helmet or a bat or a fit, the coach should put him on the bench. Parents play a big role in sportsmanship, just as in other areas. Their attitudes influence their sons' attitudes."

The president of the organization stood up. "If there

are no more questions for Dallas Stone. Thank you for coming and sharing this project with us." Dallas sat down while last minute announcements were made. As soon as the meeting adjourned, he walked quickly to Julie's table.

"What do you think?" he asked. "Are many of them for it?"

"Hard to tell. You are aware that our standing rules state that we don't contribute money to outside projects?"

"Yes, your president told me. But the committee felt every concerned person should have an opportunity to hear our facts. Your members could talk it up in the community. And some of them might want to make individual donations."

"You're a good speaker. If anyone could convince them that we need a baseball team, you could," she said sincerely.

"I'm a good speaker?" Dallas was surprised. "Did I convince you?"

"Oh, Dallas," she started and was interrupted by other women surrounding them, wanting to speak to Dallas. Julie stepped back to make room.

One elderly woman who couldn't get close to Dallas turned to Julie. "I think Dallas Stone should be the coach," she said. "My husband, rest his soul, would have been one hundred percent for this team. I want to give this contribution in his memory."

Julie glanced at the check the woman waved around. One thousand dollars! At this rate, the committee would raise the money well before the November deadline when they would present their proposition to the school board.

Dallas as the coach? The woman had an interesting idea. He had mentioned some time ago that they would be taking applications for the position soon. Although they didn't have three years' operating expenses in hand, they still needed to have a coach in mind to present to the school board. That meant the superintendent and the high school principal had to be interviewing applicants by the end of September so they could screen them and call the finalists back for a second interview.

Julie broached the subject when they were alone that evening. They had flown to Joplin to try another Chinese restaurant. The food was good, and it was nice to get out of Tribune. Wherever they went in town, they were stopped by committee supporters for an update on the fund raising. Julie couldn't believe she was going to bring up the topic herself when no one else was around to do it.

"Dallas, have you started taking applications for the coaching position?"

"Positions. We need one coach and an assistant. Yes, we advertised the positions last weekend, even though the jobs are iffy. If we don't get the team, we don't need coaches, and we want all applicants to understand that." He spooned another helping of fried rice on his plate.

"I should have shown you our ads in the newspaper. We also advertised in the Joplin and Springfield papers. Many times people wanting a job will pick up a larger paper than the *Tribune Daily* to check the opportunities. We want a good coach."

"What about you?"

"What about me?"

"Why don't you apply?"

He looked thoughtful. "It might be considered conflict of interest. Here I am heading up this project—to create a coaching position for myself? I don't know."

"No one would think that. How could they? You have a business in town. You don't need a job. And you don't need the money, as far as I can see. All they would think is that you know the game and would like to remain in it."

"Perhaps," he said noncommittally.

"Who's applied so far? Have you seen the applications?"

"No. But several names have been mentioned."

"I understand your reticence. Answer this, if you can. Has Mel Cooney applied for the job?"

He nodded. "Don't repeat that to anyone."

"I won't have to. I've heard rumors at school that he very much wants that job. He'd be the worst kind of coach. But you'd be great."

She had given it a good deal of thought since that morning when he'd spoken to her AAUW meeting. It appeared that the committee would get the money. She wasn't going to stop that. But she could influence how the program was run.

"Dallas, you'd be great." She waved her fork in the air for emphasis. "You have a teaching certificate, even though you wouldn't be teaching anything. Not that coaching isn't teaching. You know what I mean."

"Yes, I know."

"And, you have the sporting goods store. As coach, you'd only need late afternoons off. I'll bet that could be easily arranged."

"Probably," he admitted.

"You work well with kids. You'd be ideal."

"And that settles it?"

"Yes," she answered and dipped her spoon into her egg drop soup. "What do you think? Will you do it?"

"Let's just say I'll keep an open mind. What I will do, if I can, is start a Fellowship of Christian Athletes chapter in Tribune. Did you realize we don't have one at the high school?"

"I've never given it any thought," Julie admitted. "But it's a wonderful idea. I'll help if I can."

"Thanks. I've been talking to coaches in our conference and have names to contact to get a charter and all the paperwork done."

"We'll mention it in the school newspaper under club notes as soon as you have a meeting time."

"Thanks, Julie. Sometimes we make a good team."

# twelve

School had been in session for three weeks. During the last few days, the thermometer had stayed at the eighty degree mark, which made the classrooms tolerable, but uncomfortable. The teacher's lounge was air conditioned, and the teachers rushed there with their lunches and stayed until the last possible minute before getting back to their classes.

"Ah," Julie said as she and her friend Carol entered the cool room for third lunch period.

"Ah," Carol echoed. "Could I hold my afternoon classes in here?"

"You'd have to fight me for room," Julie told her.

"And the rest of us," Mel Cooney said as he picked up his tray. "Back to the heat zone." He left with the other stragglers from the second lunch period.

"Norm says he's heard that Mel Cooney will be the new baseball coach," Carol said.

"Really?" Julie asked. "I thought they hadn't made their decision yet."

"I don't think it's official. Just general consensus."

"Do you know who else has applied?"

"No. Norm can't find out much. Applications aren't going through the committee, but straight to personnel."

"I see." *So,* Julie thought, *Dallas hasn't applied.* She'd asked him several times and each time he'd said he was keeping an open mind. She was tired of the phrase.

"I'm going to attend the school board meeting," said

another teacher who had been listening to the conversation. "We need a new science lab before we need a baseball team."

"How about a computer lab?" another teacher added.

"Or a wider variety of reference books," the librarian said.

"I think we could all think of better ways to spend the money," Julie said.

"I'm surprised at you," Carol said. "With Dallas heading up the committee, I thought you'd be all for it."

"I'm keeping an open mind," Julie said and could have bit back the words as soon as she'd said them.

"The committee has twenty-three thousand dollars," Carol said. "Norm broadcasts the daily totals every morning and night. You know, see how they did each day. On days when Dallas speaks, the money comes pouring in."

"He's good," the librarian said. "I heard him at the Soroptimist meeting. He could convince snow to fall in July."

"Snow sounds wonderful," said another teacher.

"You'll sing a different tune in January," Carol said. "When it's zero outside, you'll want this heat."

Conversation turned to the weather, but Julie couldn't let go of the baseball issue. She had asked one of her sports reporters to write an unbiased piece on the baseball committee. He had turned it in that morning, but it did not present both sides of the issue. It dwelled on what the committee was doing to raise money. She'd speak with that student in her sixth period class and have him get some person-on-the-street interviews to balance the article.

She was better off remaining silent, but remaining neutral was difficult when she was pulled in both directions.

"I think Dallas should be coach," she said.

"That's a great idea. Will he do it?" Carol asked.

"I don't know. Maybe someone should talk to him. He's good with kids, and he's a good sportsman. He doesn't let winning override the character building aspects of the game. And he knows an education is more important than a sport. He's even starting a Fellowship of Christian Athletes chapter in Tribune."

"I'll see what Norm can do to convince him," Carol said. "I'll call him as soon as I eat."

The other teachers didn't comment, but looked at Julie as if she were a traitor.

"They're going to raise the money," she pointed out in self-defense. "The community is behind them. But we may be able to influence how the program is run." She repeated the logic that she had used on herself.

"We can still make a stand against them at the school board meeting. They have to convince the board that the program is needed," the librarian said. "If we unite, we'll have a better chance."

Other teachers agreed with the librarian. Julie remained quiet and finished her lunch. She left the lounge early and returned to her hot classroom.

Dallas replaced the receiver on his desk. He strode to the back of the store and found Alex in his office working on back orders.

"That was the sixth call I've had this afternoon asking me to apply for the coaching position," he announced.

"What do you think?"

"I think you'd be great."

"What about the store? I know I'm not the brains of this outfit, but I contribute."

"You do a lot for the store," Alex said. "But your contribution is in public relations and you fill in the gap when we need more sales people on the floor. How can I say this tactfully? We can do without you, Dallas."

"Thanks. It's nice to know your true worth."

"You could work mornings and spend the afternoons at the ballpark. That would be even more advertising for us. I say go for it."

Dallas nodded thoughtfully and returned to his glass office. He had talked to God about it and admitted that he wanted to do it. He wanted to coach the team he had worked so hard for. There was no doubt in his mind that they would get the team. They weren't that far from achieving their monetary goal, and by charging admission and running the snack bar, they might be able to be self-supporting after the three years had exhausted their initial funds.

Even before Julie had broached the subject, he had thought about being coach. Coaching the Legion team had been fun. The boys' enthusiasm was contagious, and he needed to remain in the game. The trip to Kansas City had reaffirmed that in his mind.

He missed baseball.

He leaned against the door frame. *Please, God, help me make the right decision,* he prayed silently.

Julie sat in the crowded stands at the American Legion baseball park with her sister. The town had turned out en masse for the exhibition game. They had never supported the Legion team as well. There were enough mothers working the concession stand so that they could be relieved every inning and still get to see a part of the fund-raising game between Gentry and Tribune.

According to Dallas, Mel Cooney had been eager for his team to play. Gentry was missing a couple of players who were off to college, but basically they were the same team that had beaten Dallas's team in the summer tournament. Julie thought that Mel wanted to play only so he could show off his coaching skills and get an edge on the other applicants. She wished Dallas would consider it. She knew pressure was being applied. Carol had Norm call him and Norm had started a "draft Dallas" campaign. But Dallas had not mentioned it to her, and she had asked so often in the past, she hated to nag him about it.

The Gentry team was good. The bad sportsmanship they had exhibited at the Springfield game was missing. Mel wanted to make a good impression.

Jimmie Madison started as pitcher. Cindy sat in the stands instead of working an early shift in the concession stand. He was taken out in the bottom of the third with two outs to go. He was wild. He'd walked three and hit a fourth on the arm, giving up a run.

Dallas put Brad Williams in to pitch. Julie had watched him in her class. He was quiet. He didn't contribute to class discussions, and the work he turned in was less than adequate. It was as if he felt inferior to the other students and was fulfilling his expectations of himself.

On the baseball field, he was a different person. He

checked all bases, then wound up and pitched. Strike. He again checked the loaded bases and picked the runner off third. Two outs. He fired the ball toward home plate. Strike two. Another pitch was low and outside. The batter swung, hit only air, and retired the side.

In the next inning, Julie watched Brad with intense concentration. He surprised her. He was in command on a ball diamond, yet he was controlled by others in a classroom. It was as if he had two personalities.

At the end of eight full innings of play, the score stood at Gentry—five, Tribune—four.

"Let's go Tribune," Julie shouted as the team ran for the dugout after holding Gentry scoreless in the top of the ninth.

Julie held her breath as the first batter struck out. The ninth batter was the pitcher, Brad Williams. He swung at the first pitch and connected. He made it to second before the ball was brought back into the infield.

The next batter hit a single, advancing Brad to third. Cleve Owens stepped up to the plate. He glanced over at Dallas, who stood in the coach's box by third base. He nodded to Dallas that he had caught the signal and faked a bunt which caused the catcher to miss the ball. The catcher flung his face mask into the dirt, but he didn't find the ball in time to keep Brad from stealing home or prevent the runner at first from advancing to second.

The fans were on their feet. The score was tied, with the winning run on second base and only one out.

Julie watched Dallas go through a serious of gestures, wondering what the sign language meant. Cleve nodded and stepped back into the batter's box. He watched two balls go by, then hit a line drive close to first. The first baseman missed the ball and Cleve flew straight past the base, turning to the left as if he were going to try for second.

The fielder threw the ball to the second baseman as a cutoff throw. Cleve kept running toward second as if he were unaware that the second baseman had the ball. All of a sudden, he changed direction and headed back for first. The second baseman threw the ball to the first baseman and they had Cleve trapped between them.

The fans from Gentry were yelling, "Home, home." Julie looked away from Cleve just in time to see the base runner cross home plate to the roar of the home crowd.

Dallas had engineered a victory. He had Cleve sacrifice an out and confuse the defense so that the winning run could score.

The Tribune players were hugging each other. Dallas gave Cleve a high five. Brad joined in the celebration as the winning pitcher. His face radiated joy. It transformed him from the quiet student to a confident ball-player.

Cindy had tears in her eyes. "We won, we won," she shouted, and Julie found herself jumping up and down with the other fans.

Half an hour after the game, stragglers still stood around the ballpark, reliving the victory. Julie helped clean up the concession stand.

An early October coolness made the stand comfortable, quite a change from the hot August afternoon she'd endured the last time she'd been in the concession stand. Wade and Norm helped load up empty canisters of pop onto the Coke truck. Cindy packed boxes of candy away.

"How's it going?" Dallas stuck his head in to the

concession stand. "Need help?"

"We're almost done," Cindy said. "Congratulations!"

"Thanks. The committee was in a win-win situation. If we lost the game, we could point out that the Gentry Legion team was also their high school team and should beat us because they've played together so much. And if we won—well, a little success goes a long way."

Dallas moved over by Julie. "What did you think?"

"It was great." She could tell by his flushed face that he was still elated by the victory. "Did you actually plan out that last play with Cleve? What was the signal you gave him?"

Dallas laughed. "You can't expect me to give away signals, Julie. Actually, that was a major mistake by ballplayers this old, but I'm glad they fell for it." He placed a hand on her shoulder and she reached up and patted it.

"Dallas?" She felt his forehead.

"Dallas Stone, you're sick. I thought you look flushed because of the excitement. You must have a high fever."

"Dallas?" Cindy said and felt his forehead, as well.

"You're going home," Julie ordered.

"I will as soon as we finish here," Dallas said.

"Now! Have you taken anything for the fever?"

"I took a couple of aspirin before the game."

"Come on," she said and put her arm around his waist urging him toward the door. "I'm driving you. Cindy, would you drop my car off at Dallas's house?" Julie turned and tossed her keys to her sister.

Dallas wanted to stay, but one look at Julie and he knew she was more determined than he. Besides, he felt awful.

"I can drive," he said.

"No," Julie said and took his keys out of his hand.

"Is that your mean teacher voice?" he tried to joke.

"I'm not a mean teacher. Just firm."

Thankful that his car had an automatic shift, Julie put it into gear and started for Winfield Avenue.

"Do you have 7-Up at home?"

"You thirsty?" Julie wasn't making much sense to him.

"No. You're going to drink it."

"I don't know if there's any or not." He leaned his head against the headrest and closed his eyes.

"If not, I'll get some while you're lying down." She pressed the garage door opener as they neared his house and smoothly drove the car inside.

Dallas felt terrible. Adrenaline alone had kept him on his feet through the game. Now that he had given into it, the heat seemed to overtake his body.

Julie opened his car door and helped him into the house.

"A tepid bath would make you feel better," she said. "Do you think you can manage?"

"Sure," he said and sat down hard on the couch.

Julie swung his feet up and propped a pillow behind his head. She disappeared for a moment and he heard water running. When she returned, she took his shoes and socks off.

"Come on," she said and helped him to his feet. "Can you manage the rest?"

"Yeah."

"Where are your pajamas?"

"Pajamas? Uh, second drawer at the back."

Julie left him in the bathroom and went to the first bedroom. It had an unlived-in look. She went to the second door and found his room. She discovered five pairs of pajamas in the second drawer of the chest of drawers. All were in their original packaging. She shook a blue pair out of its bag and took out the straight pins.

Knocking on the bathroom door, she called, "They're outside the door. Just reach out for them when you're ready. Are you all right?"

"I'm okay."

By the time Cindy pulled into the driveway with Julie's car, Dallas was in bed asleep. Julie went outside to meet her so she wouldn't ring the doorbell and wake him up. Wade and their boys pulled up right behind Cindy.

"His fever is almost a hundred and four. I can't believe he came to that game," Julie told them.

"He's stubborn," Cindy said and handed Julie her keys. "Do you need anything? 7-Up?"

"Dallas had never heard of drinking 7-Up when you're running a fever. Can you believe it?"

"He hasn't been around Mom enough, that's all," Cindy said. "I take it you need some?"

Julie nodded. "That and aspirin. He has two aspirins left in one of those flat tin containers. He says he doesn't get sick."

"I'll go," Wade said and took the boys with him.

Julie and Cindy checked on Dallas, but he was still asleep.

"He's had a tepid bath. Do you think I should call a doctor?" Julie asked.

"I'd wait awhile. It's probably just a bug. Dallas has

been burning the candle at both ends. Working at the store and raising money for the committee. He's talked to every group in town and then some. He's busy day and night. The guy's worn out."

They waited for Wade's return. Cindy sat on the couch. Julie paced back and forth, occasionally tiptoeing to the bedroom to check on Dallas.

"Calm down, Julie. He's got a bug. He'll be fine."

"I'm calm. I'm just concerned," Julie said and sat down in a chair, only to pop back up again and dash outside as Wade pulled into the driveway.

"Will you be all right here?" Cindy asked as she climbed into the passenger seat of Wade's car.

"I'll be fine. Well, thanks for bringing the supplies and my car," she told her family and waved goodbye.

Julie carried the supplies into the kitchen and put the 7-Up into the refrigerator. A phone call to Marti arranged for her and Hal to spend the night with Dallas.

"He'll probably argue," Julie said, "but I'll tell him it's all arranged and you'll be here after your dinner party."

Julie wandered the house after talking to Dallas's sister. She perused the bookshelves, selected a book, and settled into the overstuffed chair in Dallas's room to read. She felt better when she was with him instead of being in another area of the house. She read for a few minutes but couldn't get involved in the book.

Dallas stirred, and Julie walked over to his bed. She took his warm hand in hers.

"I'm here, Dallas," she whispered to the sleeping man.

She picked up the well-worn Bible from his bedside stand and returned to the chair.

"Please take care of him, Lord," she whispered and turned to read her favorite Psalms.

## thirteen

Dallas woke up to find himself in blue pajamas and in his own bed. His head hurt and after a moment he remembered that Julie had brought him home from the game.

"Julie?" he said in a low voice. A movement caught his eye. She was getting up from the chair by the window.

"How're you feeling? I want to check your temperature before you have a drink. It's time to take aspirin again." She stuck a thermometer in his mouth so that he couldn't answer her question. "I'll be right back with some 7-Up."

When she returned, she read the thermometer and helped him sit up so he could drink. His mouth was dry and the liquid felt good on his throat.

"One hundred two. Much better, but not good," she said. "Take these aspirins."

He swallowed them as she directed, noticing that the concern in her eyes belied her efficient manner. He looked over at his alarm clock. The digital display read 7:42. "I've been asleep several hours?"

"Yes. And it was the best thing for you. Now where do you hurt, other than your head?"

"That's all." He started to throw off the blankets so he could get up.

"Oh, no, you don't," Julie said. "You're staying in bed. Tomorrow you might get to lie on the couch, if you're good. What do you feel like eating?"

"Sweet–and–sour pork."

"You must be feeling better. But you're getting chicken noodle soup."

"Why'd you ask if you'd already decided?"

Julie smiled. "If your request had been reasonable, I might have considered it as an alternative to the Russell Sickness Cure. No matter what the ailment, 7-Up and chicken noodle soup will fix you up. Be back in a minute."

She returned with soup and crackers on a tray and perched on the bed to watch him eat.

"Is it all right? Not too hot?"

"It's perfect and it does taste good. There might be something to this Russell Sickness Cure."

"Oh, there is." She leaned down and kissed him on the cheek.

"You can do better than that for a sick man," he said and puckered up.

"Oh, no," she said and laughed. "Germs."

Dallas felt better after he'd eaten. Julie fluffed his pillows, turned on the bedroom TV, and moved a chair over by the bed.

They watched a movie, with Julie freshening Dallas's 7-Up during commercials.

He reached for her hand. She brought his hand up to her lips and kissed it.

"Beneath that very efficient facade lies a tender woman," Dallas said softly.

Julie smiled. "Remember that old teacher's adage, 'Don't smile until Christmas'? I took that to heart. Because most of my students are taller than I am, I need to establish that I'm the boss from day one. At the first of the year, I tend to get carried away, but so far I've had no discipline problems."

"I'll bet you're a great teacher. Wish I'd had someone like you when I was in high school."

"She would have found you charming."

"Me? Charming?"

Julie couldn't help herself. She placed her hand against the side of his face and leaned down to kiss him.

"No, Julie," Dallas said and turned his head so that she kissed his cheek. "You were right before—germs. As much as I'd like to kiss you, I don't want you getting sick."

She nodded. "You just look so kissable like this."

"Hold on to that thought. I'll be well soon."

She touched his cheek again. "You're hotter." She checked his temperature. "It's gone up, and it's not time for aspirin yet."

"I'm all right. Just stay here by me."

They watched the news.

"I called your sister while you were asleep. She didn't think you had a doctor here."

"Marti's right. I don't need a doctor. I'll be all right. I've just got some bug."

"I know," Julie agreed. But she was worried. "Do you think you could sleep now? You could take some aspirin a bit early."

"All right." He downed the aspirin and Julie rearranged his pillows.

"Good night, Dallas," she said and kissed him in a safe area.

"You'll be here tomorrow?" he asked.

"Yes. I'll check on you before I go," she said, but she

had no intention of leaving until Marti and Hal arrived.

Julie quietly cleaned up the kitchen. Dallas was asleep when she checked on him, but he felt even hotter.

She sat back down in the chair to watch him sleep, but was only there a moment when she heard a car in the driveway. With quiet, hurried steps, she reached the front door before Marti rang the bell.

"Come in," she said softly. "Dallas is asleep."

Hal carried in a suitcase.

"Across town and we need to pack," he said.

"Oh, you needed your toothbrush, too," Marti said and patted her husband on the back. "How's he doing?"

"His fever's back up. He can have more aspirin around three, if he wakes up."

"Okay. We'll take over. Why don't you come over for breakfast, say around eight?"

"I'll be here," Julie said. "Call if you need anything."


Dallas was sick for three days. Julie spent Sunday afternoon with him and stopped by on her way to school on Monday. When she returned to his house Monday evening, he was dressed, and her mother had been by.

"I'm never going to eat chicken noodle soup again," Dallas declared. "Although today's lunch was the best. Real chicken and homemade noodles. Your mom's a good cook. But I'm going to have Chinese for supper," he said. He had put up with constant babying from Julie, Marti, Cindy, and now her mother. Enough was enough.

"Fine. I'll go get it," Julie said.

"No. We'll go out and eat. I'm getting cabin fever. And I'm going to work tomorrow. No debates."

"Let me check your temperature."

"No. It's fine. I'm normal. I had a bug and now it's gone." He stood up and hugged her to him. He held her close for a moment before he lowered his head to kiss her. His lips caressed hers in a kiss she felt clear to her toes.

"See, no germs," he said when he pulled back.

Julie didn't care if she got a fever of one hundred six. It would be worth it for that kiss.

"Let's go eat," Dallas said. "I'm starved for fried rice."

He seemed to be fine and insisted on driving.

"I've prowled the house today, to get strength back," he explained over dinner. "And I got some work done on the Fellowship of Christian Athletes. I made a few phone calls. Our organizational meeting will be held a week from this Saturday. The paperwork came in today's mail, so I have the forms to apply for a charter. I called John and reserved the electric company meeting room."

"Is a weekend a good time for this? I thought you'd have it at the high school during the week."

Dallas's grin looked like the cat who ate the canary.

"I've got three Kansas City baseball players coming for the meeting. I also thought we'd open it up to the public. This is not just a high school club. The men who play slow pitch softball can come, too."

"So, you've decided to involve the community," Julie said thoughtfully. "That's a good move. What about women and our high school girls?"

"They're welcome, too. We want to foster good relations between all the teams at the high school, both girls and boys."

He took a big bite of sweet–and–sour pork. "Boy, does this tastes good," he said and concentrated for a moment on eating.

Julie pulled a small note pad and pen from her purse. She wrote the place and date of the meeting.

"What time is the meeting?"

"Two in the afternoon. I know the kids have Saturday night dates, and I wouldn't want to interfere with that," he said and raised and lowered his eyebrows in a playful manner.

"You're definitely feeling better," Julie said and laughed. "I was thinking about signs for the school. You could use a few posters scattered about. A couple by the cafeteria, in the gym, in the locker rooms, by the library. And a notice for the bulletin board. We can get Mr. Kellough to announce it over the PA system during seventh period on the Friday before the meeting." She wrote in her notebook as she talked. "Who are your special guests?"

Dallas put down his fork and gave her his whole attention.

"Actually, that's where you come into play, Julie."

"Oh?"

"J.J. and Kelli are coming with their two kids. They'll stay overnight at my house. The other guys are single. Don Wingate and Steve Eddgar. They're going to drive down and back to Kansas City on that Saturday." He paused.

"And?" Julie had no idea where he was leading, but his reluctance to get to the point was beginning to make her edgy.

"So, I have a favor to ask."

"And that is...?"

"I was hoping you'd want to entertain Kelli and the kids while J.J. and I are at the meeting."

"That's it?"

"Yeah. You've met Kelli. She's quite a gal. And the kids are okay. And you're good with kids," he said.

"Dallas, I'd be happy to help out. I like Kelli. Does she have boys or girls? I could take them out to the farm. You know, show the city kids some cows and horses."

"They have two daughters. I can't remember their ages, but I think the older one is in school now."

"No problem. What about dinner that night? Have you made plans?"

"I thought we could get a baby sitter and take Kelli and J.J. out to eat, maybe take Marti and Hal, too. Do you know any baby sitters?"

"I'll bet Cindy would watch the kids. I'll take care of that end of it."

"Thanks, Julie. I'll concentrate on the meeting, and you can concentrate on being hostess. I owe you one for this," he said.

Julie got a mischievous look in her eyes. "Now that you bring it up, I could use a favor, too."

"Oh?"

"Are you through eating? We need to get you back home so you can rest."

Dallas stood up and pulled her chair out for her.

"I'm fine. I was going to suggest a walk around the square. I need to regain strength. Lying around is what zaps the energy right out of you." He paid the bill and led her outside.

Julie pushed up the sleeves of her cotton sweater. Indian summer had made a late appearance. It was the first part of October and the leaves on the trees around the court house had begun to turn brilliant colors. Some drifted down in the still air as the couple walked slowly around the square.

"So, Julie, what favor do you need?" Dallas sounded as apprehensive as she had felt when he was asking her about playing hostess for him.

"It's nothing terrible," she quickly reassured him. "Would you be an usher with me at the play on Friday and Saturday nights and Sunday afternoon?"

"What play? What does an usher do?"

"It's a long story," Julie said. "But the job's simple. All you do is pass out programs and direct people to empty seats. It would actually be a high profile time for you. Get you in front of the public again. Maybe bring in some money for the committee," she added to persuade him.

"And you're doing it, too?"

"Oh, yes. I'll be right beside you." They had been walking with her hand in the crook of his arm. Now she reached for his hand and squeezed it.

"All right, I'll help you."

"Thanks. This means a lot to me, Dallas. You're actually helping my old drama teacher."

"What's the play?"

*"A Midsummer Night's Dream."*

"Shakespeare?"

"Yes. It's from his youthful period of poetic fantasy."

"Isn't this a little late for a midsummer play?"

"You're right. That's part of the long story. Let's go

over and sit on that bench," she suggested, wanting Dallas not to overdo it on his first day up and about.

They crossed the street to the courthouse lawn, sat on an empty bench, and watched the traffic go around the square.

Julie cleared her throat. "My old drama teacher called me at school today. She's directing the play for the Tribune Little Theater. It was originally scheduled for August, but Mrs. Cooney broke her leg and was in the hospital in traction for two weeks. The cast didn't think they knew the blocking and interpretation of lines well enough to continue rehearsals without her. Mrs. Cooney is quite a Shakespeare buff," she explained.

"Well, by the time Mrs. Cooney was able to use crutches, a month had gone by and they needed the time to get their act together, such as it is. They thought of canceling this production and moving on to another play, but decided they could do it indoors as well as in the park around the lake.

"So, then they had to come up with a stage set. All and all, it's taken longer than they anticipated. But now they're ready and in need of support people. Which is where you and I come in. I've ushered for them before."

"I take it you like this Mrs. Cooney?"

"One of the best teachers I've ever had. She's retired now, but is still as much a character as she was when I had her. She made school fun and a learning experience at the same time. But she wasn't a person you ever crossed."

"Ready to walk on?" Dallas asked. He took her hand again and they completed their round of the square before driving back to his home.

"Want to come in for a cup of coffee?" he suggested after he had parked his car in the garage.

"Thanks, but I've got to grade some papers. We're starting research projects, and I've got to hand their preliminary outlines back to the students tomorrow. I'll walk you in, though."

"Sort of like escorting me home after a date," Dallas said and laughed.

"That's right." She fell right in with his idea. She reached across the car and patted him on the arm. "Stay right there."

After climbing out on her side, Julie walked around to Dallas's door and opened it, offering her hand to help him out.

She walked him to the kitchen door.

"I had a wonderful time tonight," Dallas said and stood beside the door, waiting.

"Me, too," Julie said. She stood straight with her arms at her sides.

"This is where you give me the good night kiss," Dallas said.

"I know. I'm trying to figure out how to do it." Since he towered over her, she would have to pull him down to her height.

"It's not hard," Dallas teased. "Believe me, I'll cooperate."

"I didn't doubt that for a minute." Julie reached up for his shoulders and hooked a hand around his neck. "Come here, you big lug."

Dallas had had all the play acting he could handle. He pulled Julie into his arms and initiated a kiss of his own. It was another of those toe-curling kisses that sent

Julie's heart soaring. Julie kissed him back again and again.

"I guess you'd better go in," she said breathlessly.

"I guess so. Sure you can't come in?" Dallas asked and winked.

"I'm sure. I'll call you," Julie said, keeping up their pretense.

"Good night," Dallas called.

Julie walked out of the garage and climbed into her own car. Back at her duplex she realized she hadn't told Dallas when to report for usher duty. With a light heart, she looked up his number, and found it wasn't in the phone book. She hadn't called him before. His number might be unlisted. She dialed information and found it was a new listing that hadn't been included.

After sticking the number on the bulletin board beside her phone, she dialed Dallas. He answered on the second ring.

"I missed you," she said without identifying herself.

"Me, too," he said. "These have been the longest fifteen minutes of my life."

Julie laughed and asked him to report to the municipal auditorium by six-thirty on Friday night.

"Why don't I pick you up first and we'll get a bite to eat? Is this a formal event?"

"No. A tie and a sport coat will be fine. No suit or tux required," she explained.

"Okay. I'll pick you up at five-thirty and I'll call you before then. Good night, Julie."

"Good night, Dallas," she said softly and hung up the phone.

What was it about that man that made her heart race?

She knew he didn't want to usher at the theater, but he had agreed to help. And she knew he wasn't thrilled about seeing *A Midsummer Night's Dream,* either. *He's doing it for me,* she thought.

What did he really think about her? She had already admitted to herself that she loved him. She wanted to be with him. But how did he feel about her?

In words, he had never told her. Except that time he had admitted that he'd had to research Harold Pinter and wanted to impress her with his knowledge. In actions, he had told her over and over that he liked her. Going to family Sunday dinners with her, going to the symphony, taking her to meet his family, and now ushering at the play—all said he cared. But how much?

"Lord," she prayed. "If it is Your will, please have him love me, too."

By five-thirty on Friday, Julie was dressed in a burgundy dress and ready for the evening at the theater. She hadn't seen Dallas since Monday, although they had talked on the phone every night.

When he arrived, she tried to be cool and calm. But the moment he opened his arms, she flew into them and rested her head against his chest. This was where she belonged.

Dallas hugged her to him and felt, as he did whenever he was around her, that she was his kindred spirit. He could have held her forever, but she pushed away from his chest and looked up at him with those bright eyes.

"I guess we'd better get going so we can get to the theater on time."

"I guess so," he agreed reluctantly.

They grabbed a sandwich at the sub shop and made it to the theater with plenty of time to spare.

Dallas hadn't been around a play production before. Oh, he'd attended a few in his high school and college days, but he'd never watched a play if he didn't know one of the actors.

The activity backstage was frantic. Actors darted here and there looking for props. The stage hands were raising and lowering scenery.

Julie introduced Dallas to Mrs. Cooney, who was nothing like what he had imagined. Although she was a petite woman, probably five–two or so, and had the gray hair and wrinkles of a seventy-year-old woman, those were the only features that matched his mental image of her. She barked, she yelled, and she waved her arms around.

"I told you she made school fun," Julie reminded him.

"Yes, but you didn't say she was a miniature Attila the Hun."

"Good description. I always thought of her as Napoleon," Julie said and laughed. "We'd better take our places and get out of the way. Opening night jitters must have hold of everyone."

They made their way to the front of the municipal auditorium and picked up a stack of programs.

"The tickets have seat numbers on them," Julie explained. "This starts with row one and all the seats are assigned letters."

"Just like at a ball stadium."

"Exactly. We just don't have box seats. If you run into a problem, ask me. I thought there would be another usher, but it may be just the two of us. I'll stand over by that aisle and you take this one. If their letter comes after L, make them come over to my aisle."

"I think I've got this. Are we expecting a big crowd?" he asked as they walked to the back of the auditorium.

"I don't know. Usually the Little Theater has community support. We have tomorrow night and Sunday afternoon to go. Some people might wait for the review in tomorrow's paper before they decide to come. This is also the first Shakespeare they've attempted. So, I can't even guess how many will show up."

They stood together for another few minutes until some early arrivals needed to be seated. Less than an hour later, they stood at the back of the auditorium as the lights dimmed and the curtain went up.

"Let's sit back here until we're needed. During intermission, we may have to help some back to their seats," Julie whispered.

Dallas sat down beside her in the last row and slipped his arm around her. There were plenty of seats to choose from. Probably half the auditorium was empty. He hadn't seen many people he knew. This was not the regular baseball committee crowd. He did see the president of the school board, although he didn't know it was her until Julie had pointed her out.

The play, a fantasy of leaping men and women frolicking beside a lake made of slanted mirrors, almost put Dallas to sleep. When the soldiers began dancing with the Amazon women, he nudged Julie.

"This is Shakespeare at his best?" he whispered.

"Well, fantasy isn't for everyone," she whispered back. "Personally, I like his tragedies better."

He was delighted when the play was over. He walked with Julie backstage to congratulate the actors and Mrs. Cooney, but his heart wasn't in it. Maybe they would get better by the afternoon performance on Sunday. He certainly hoped so.

He smiled at Julie and suggested they get an ice cream cone at the local parlor where the proprietor made his own ice cream. There had to be a highlight to the evening, and Dallas thought even vanilla would be more exciting than the play.

On Saturday night, Dallas dressed with care and showed up at Julie's around six-thirty. They had decided to eat after the performance. He was hoping they could sneak out before the end of the play. But Julie thought it would be rude not to greet the cast after the final bow. So, again, he squirmed in his chair and watched the actors prance on stage.

By Sunday, the thought of going back to the auditorium made Dallas want to scream, but he held his tongue all through church, through Julie's class, and even at the Russell's Sunday dinner.

"That's mighty nice of you to help her out this way," Charles Russell told Dallas after they had eaten dinner and he and Julie were preparing to go to the theater for the final time.

"Well, she's pretty special," Dallas said, wishing Julie would hurry up and find her purse so they could be on their way and get the performance over with.

"It doesn't take women long to get us where they want us," Merle said in a little aside to Dallas. "You'd better watch out."

"Yeah," John Russell added. "She's got you at the

theater now. What's next? The ballet or a poetry reading?" The men all laughed while Dallas counted to ten.

"I've dragged her to plenty of ball games, so I guess it's turn around time." Julie came out of the kitchen in time to catch the last of his words, and she beamed at him.

"We compromise," she announced to her brothers and father. "Ready, Dallas?"

He wanted to be with her, just not at the theater. He wondered if she would object to the portable radio and headset he had stuck in the car. No one would see them. He'd go get them after the play had begun. He just couldn't sit through another two hours of romping on stage.

Dallas began his ushering duties and seated two of his American Legion ball players. They looked as shocked to see him as he was to see them.

"Miss Russell's giving us extra credit if we come see this," Brad Williams confided in him.

"I'll make sure she sees you," Dallas assured them. That sort of effort needed to be rewarded.

Dallas was just seating an elderly couple near the front when Mrs. Cooney climbed down the side steps of the stage and motioned to him. He looked around to see if she was looking at someone else, but it appeared that he was the one she wanted.

"You'll have to come back stage. We have a problem," she said in what was a low voice for her. Dallas was sure she could be heard by at least the first eight rows.

He walked swiftly to her side. "May I help you?" he asked.

"We need you back stage," she said and turned and climbed back up the steps.

Dallas looked at Julie, who was at the rear of the auditorium talking to a young couple, but he couldn't grab her attention.

"Come on." Mrs. Cooney's voice was beginning to reach her normal booming level.

Dallas scurried up the steps and disappeared behind the curtain.

"What is it? What's wrong?"

"You'll have to take Sam's place. He's in the bathroom sicker than a dog. The costume's in the green room."

"Oh, no, Mrs. Cooney," Dallas protested. "I'm no actor."

She gave him a leveling look that he was sure had terrified her most belligerent student. "We have no choice. The show must go on. You have no lines. All you have to do is watch the other soldiers."

"Soldiers! Wear a dress and dance with an Amazon! No way, Mrs. Cooney. I've done all I can stand just to watch this play for two nights."

Mrs. Cooney drew herself up to her full five–feet–two inches and announced, "And I thought you were worthy of Julie Russell."

Julie looked around the auditorium and couldn't find Dallas anywhere. The last she had seen of him he was taking an elderly couple to the front row. It was almost curtain time. Perhaps he had slipped out to the car to get his Walkman. She had seen the radio in the back seat of the car and knew that if possible, he was going to block out the play by listening to music or a football game.

The lights flickered then dimmed. Julie walked out into the lobby to look around. No Dallas. She stepped outside, but he wasn't anywhere around his car. Maybe he had gone to the men's room.

She took her customary seat in the back row and hoped he would join her. She didn't watch the play; she felt she could recite the lines by now and do a better job of it than the actors. Minutes passed and he didn't appear. Julie walked back out into the lobby and asked the woman in the ticket booth if she had seen Dallas. She hadn't. The woman in the refreshment booth hadn't seen him either. Julie walked outside one more time.

What could have happened to him? *Dear God, please help me find him,* she prayed silently.

Julie reluctantly walked back into the auditorium and glanced at the stage. There, towering over the other soldiers, was Dallas Stone, decked out in tights and a costume that caught him at mid-thigh.

Julie gasped. Someone nearby shushed her.

Hypnotized by the sight, Julie plopped down in an empty seat and watched the soldiers dance around. She had no idea Dallas was so nimble. She had no idea that Dallas would actually put on a costume that he had called a dress just the night before and parade across the stage. How could this happen?

When the soldiers danced with the Amazons, Julie wished she had been in the front row. Dallas's expression was murderous. Julie smothered a giggle.

At the end of the production, the cast came out for a final bow. Julie's hands hurt from clapping so hard for Dallas. As soon as the lights came up, she rushed backstage. She caught Dallas as he was trying to make a getaway to the men's dressing room.

"You were marvelous. How did this happen? I had no idea where you had gone."

Dallas was beyond humiliation.

"Let me change and we'll get out of here."

"Don't you want to go to the cast party?"

"No," Dallas growled and pushed open the dressing room door. He disappeared inside.

Julie cornered Mrs. Cooney.

"How did you get Dallas on stage?" she demanded.

Mrs. Cooney smiled slyly. "He did it for you," was all she said.

## fourteen

"I don't want to talk about it," Dallas said again, then proceeded to talk about it. "It was the most humiliating, embarrassing thing I've ever done in my entire life. And a couple of my ballplayers were in the audience. You'd better give Brad Williams and Jeff McCord extra, extra credit for sitting through that."

"Brad needs the extra credit," Julie said, trying to steer the conversation in another direction. Dallas had paced her apartment and was still upset over his acting debut. Julie tried to get him to see the humorous side, but decided it would be a few years before enough time had passed for him to laugh about it.

"I thought you might call your Legion ballplayers and tell them about the Fellowship of Christian Athletes meeting. They could spread the word for you in addition to the posters. Oh, I bought the poster board. Want to work on them?"

"How about tomorrow night?" Dallas said. "I'm going to go to the gym and work out." He figured that was an excellent way of working off his aggression.

"Good idea. Why don't you come over after work and have dinner with me. Then we'll tackle the posters."

Dallas nodded and headed toward the door.

"Dallas."

He paused with his hand on the door knob. Julie walked over to him and rested her hands on his chest.

"I can't tell you how much I appreciate your ushering with me and especially replacing the sick soldier. That took a lot of courage. And I admire you for it."

"You're welcome," he said gruffly and leaned down and tenderly kissed her on the cheek before he left.

Julie smiled to herself. That man cared about her. He hadn't said it in words, but today's actions screamed it.

She looked heavenward. "Thank you, Lord. Now I know he loves me."

With the Fellowship of Christian Athletes meeting less than a week away, Julie threw herself into organizing her time with Dallas's guests. She arranged for Cindy to watch J.J.'s daughters and borrowed some toys and games to have at Dallas's house for them to play with. She called for reservations at Hidden Acres, the best steak house in town, and she arranged for Marti and Hal to meet them there.

Dallas arrived for dinner on Monday night in a much better mood than when he had left Julie on Sunday, and together they worked on posters. Julie took them to school the next morning and conned her nephew Jimmie into putting them up.

Dallas called his Legion players and drummed up support for the meeting. He even read a public service announcement on the radio. When Saturday arrived, everything was in place. Julie was busy in Dallas's kitchen arranging a tray of cookies and brownies.

Don Wingate and Steve Eddgar arrived first. Both men were friendly to Julie. Dallas responded to their innocent flirting by sitting beside Julie and casually putting his arm on the couch behind her, giving them the signal that she was not a casual date, but someone special to him.

J.J. and Kelli arrived with their two daughters a half hour later. Julie discovered that Rhea was in kindergarten and Haley had just celebrated her second birthday. After they had unloaded suitcases in the spare bedroom and enjoyed coffee with the men, Julie whisked Kelli and the two girls out to her car.

"I thought we'd let them catch up on old news and arrange today's meeting while we have fun," she explained to Kelli. She drove them out to the farm and showed the girls the farm animals, then took them back to her duplex for lunch.

"I figured eating at home might be easier than eating out with the girls," Julie said.

"You're right. How do you know so much about kids?"

"Lots of nephews and nieces and many hours in the baby-sitting department." Julie uncovered a tray of deli meats and cheeses and wasn't surprised to see the girls eat what Kelli called "sandwiches without bread."

After lunch they put Haley down for a nap and let Rhea watch the video of *Beauty and the Beast,* which Julie had borrowed from her sister-in-law. Kelli and Julie sat at the kitchen table with cups of coffee before them.

"You're nothing like the others," Kelli commented.

"The others?" Julie questioned, but thought she knew where the conversation was headed.

"The other women Dallas has dated."

"Oh?" Julie knew she shouldn't encourage this conversation, but she was curious to know about Dallas's past.

"There was never a serious relationship that I know

of. His last girlfriend was an airline flight attendant. She was quite nice. I liked her, but there wasn't the attraction that I sense between you and Dallas." She nervously twisted some wisps of red hair between her fingers. "What are your intentions toward him?"

Julie couldn't believe what she was hearing.

"You sound like one of my brothers quizzing Dallas."

Kelli laughed. "It does sound bizarre, but I really care about Dallas. He's been a good friend to J.J. and me. I think this relationship could be serious, and I don't want him hurt."

"I hope our relationship is serious, but we haven't talked about a future, if that's what you mean."

"Sometimes men can be slow," Kelli said and shook her head. "I practically had to propose to J.J. myself, but he finally came around." She chuckled, then her expression sombered.

"What I really need to know, and you can tell me it's none of my business, is if you love Dallas."

"I love Dallas," Julie stated simply. "And I think he loves me."

"Oh, I know that," Kelli said. "He talks to J.J. and J.J. talks to me. I don't mean to be a gossip, and he didn't say it was confidential, but sometimes men need a push. And you should know where you stand."

"Thanks," Julie said.

"Dallas is serious about this Fellowship of Christian Athletes chapter. He's been a strong Christian for as long as I've known him."

"He's helped me with my Sunday school class," Julie said.

Kelli's lips parted in a wide smiled. "I think I know

all I need to know about you two, and I predict many years of happiness to come."

"Well, we'll see what the future brings." Julie didn't want to dwell on the future, although she had to admit she had considered marriage. She'd caught herself doodling "Mrs. Dallas Stone" and "Mrs. Julie Stone," on a note pad like a high school girl.

"Just don't let him be too shy about it," Kelli said.

"Speaking of shy," Julie said to change the subject, "one of Dallas's Legion ballplayers is in my classroom and never speaks. I saw him in an exhibition game, and he was like a different person. Do any of the Royals players have that type of Jekyll and Hyde personality? Is this a baseball characteristic?"

"Can't think of anyone like that," Kelli said.

"I think I'll do some investigating," Julie said. "Maybe read up on shyness." Her train of thought was interrupted by the jangle of the phone. Dallas and the other men were back at his home.

After Haley woke up, Julie and Kelli loaded up the girls and took them back to Dallas's house. The men called their meeting an unqualified success.

The entire weekend was a great success, including the dinner at Hidden Acres. Julie and Kelli didn't have another chance to talk privately, but Kelli's smile assured Julie that she had a new friend.


On Monday, Julie asked her nephew to stay a minute after class.

"How well do you know Brad Williams?" she asked.

"I played baseball with him," Jimmie said. "He barely talks to me in school. He's pretty quiet. But he's a great ballplayer. In command, somehow."

His opinion matched hers exactly. Julie asked other teachers about Brad and discovered he bordered on abnormal shyness, which explained his reluctance to participate in class discussions.

"I'm going to call Brad Williams in," Julie told Dallas that evening. "He's got a D in English. I don't understand him." She explained her mixed feelings toward the boy.

"Of course, I've only seen him on the playing field, but he's a friendly sort then, seems intelligent enough. You know," Dallas said thoughtfully, "he didn't come to that pizza party I had for the team last summer. But he came Saturday to our organizational meeting. He talked to J.J. quite a while after we dismissed. He didn't seem shy then."

"That's good, but he was probably talking baseball. If he doesn't improve in English, he won't be playing for the school team, should there be one."

"I'll talk to him, if you'd like."

"No. I'm his teacher. I want him to feel comfortable enough with me to talk in class."

The next day, Julie called Brad in. He sat at a desk and looked down at the graffiti that had been carved on it through the years. Julie explained about his grade and that part of it was based on class participation.

"If you don't understand the subject, ask questions. You must have a C average to participate in sports. I know you're hoping there will be a baseball team. I'll bet you'd like to pitch for Tribune High. Use some of that enthusiasm you feel for baseball in the classroom. If you need outside help, I'm here until four every day.

Come by and we'll talk. All right?"

He looked up at her for the first time. "Okay."

"Brad, I saw you pitch against Gentry. You were terrific."

"Thanks, Miss Russell." He grinned and his eyes lit up. "I want to pitch in the majors like Dallas Stone and J.J."

"I'd say you have a good chance. But first you have to succeed in high school. I understand concentrating on what you're good at. We all do that. It's a very normal thing to do. But we have to strive for balance. Like Dallas Stone."

"Okay, I'll try," Brad said.

After he left, something niggled at Julie. She reflected on their conversation, replaying it in her mind.

"I understand concentrating on what you're good at. We all do that." Had she actually ended a sentence with a preposition? How should she have stated it?

"We all concentrate on the area in which we excel," she said out loud, rephrasing her statement.

"We all do that," she said slowly. "We use the special talents God has given us."

Julie jumped to her feet and walked to the window then back to her desk. Her brothers had excelled in sports. She had excelled in academics. They had all concentrated on the area in which they excelled.

"Strive for balance," she said and realized that she had failed at that. Her brothers had achieved more balance than she had. Sure they watched sports in their free time, but they also held down nonsports jobs and were responsible citizens of Tribune. Her job was tied to her area of excellence, academics.

*Oh, dear God, I have been so blind. Is this Your sign to me? Did You send Brad Williams to teach me this lesson?* Julie remembered the sermon on tolerance that she had heard in Kentucky. Tolerance, balance, acceptance of others.

*Thank You, Lord. Sometimes I'm a slow learner.*

The next morning in English class, Julie called on Brad. He answered in a low voice, but he answered. The next day he showed up at her desk after the last bell.

"I don't like this literature stuff we're studying."

"The unit on the essence of an American?"

"I don't know 'essence.' "

"It's all that makes a thing what it is. Its nature. What's the essence of baseball, Brad? What's its nature?"

He shrugged. "Like playing hard?"

"Yes, that's part of it. What else does baseball mean to you?"

"Pitching right down the alley."

"Good. What else?"

He scratched his head. "Working as a team?"

"Exactly. We're studying the rugged individualism of Walt Whitman because being an American means we can be individuals as long as we don't infringe on the rights of another individual. Henry David Thoreau marched to a different drummer. He had the right to be an individual, not be like everyone else in the crowd. Just as you are an individual when you're up at bat, but a part of a unit when you're on the field. Am I making any sense?"

"I guess. I'll have to think on it."

"Do that. Read tomorrow's assignment  and concentrate on what is the nature of being an American. After class discussion, if you need to, drop by after school."

"Okay. Thanks."


"He talked to me," Julie told Dallas on the phone that night. "He actually made the overture. We didn't talk for long, but it was a beginning."

"Good. He'd better bring that grade up. I'm counting on him as a pitcher this spring."

"You're counting on him? Does that mean you're thinking of applying for coach?"

"Oh, Julie. I did apply. I didn't want to tell you because I don't want you to get your hopes up. I may not get the job."

"Yes, you will."

"There you go, doing it. Believing it's already a fact when it's very uncertain. Remember, that position has been advertised in other towns, too."

"I won't be disappointed. Where are you speaking tonight?" she asked as she toyed with the phone cord.

"Nowhere. It's just a committee meeting to see how we're doing. Keep everyone informed of progress. We're almost there."

"I didn't hear. How did we do at the game Saturday?"

"Over a thousand dollars. The town's behind this project. We're going to get a team, and the town will continue to support it by attending games. It's not just a school team. It's for the community."

"I know," Julie said and meant it. "Have a good meeting and I'll see you tomorrow night."

Julie's new attitude toward sports crystallized the day she had her talk with Brad. She credited God for showing her how sports could help a person overcome problems. She also thanked God daily for bringing Dallas Stone into her life. For her attitude had gradually changed as she had learned and understood what baseball meant to Dallas. She didn't hate sports anymore. She actually saw a place for them. They were overemphasized. That opinion had not changed, but she did see that a baseball team at the school was not a bad idea.

How the team was handled would make the difference. It certainly was an incentive for Brad. She knew it would be a long time before Brad could overcome his shyness. He was trying because of his love for baseball.

Dallas had reported that Brad was opening up in the Fellowship of Christian Athletes meetings. They had only met one more time, but Brad had stood up for his beliefs when questioned about them, a sure sign that he was trying to be more outgoing.

Dallas would be an exceptional coach. Julie didn't doubt that. His win-loss record might not be the greatest, but he cared about the players. He would shape their attitudes toward schoolwork and sportsmanship in a manner that Julie could approve of. He would guide positive responses from the spectators.

She also knew he needed baseball. Getting to handle balls, bats, and gloves in a sporting goods store was not the same as being in the game. Coaching wasn't playing, but it was the next best thing.

Julie had done her best with the baseball article in the school newspaper. Since it was a community effort, she gave it a page one headline, then continued the article on the sports page. It was fair and as unbiased as it could be. They ran negative reactions garnered from their person-on-the-street interviews, but because only one in three responses had been negative, that ratio was reflected in the article.

Julie didn't tell Dallas about her change of heart, but she supported him in his efforts—much like a Christian striving to live a righteous life as an example instead of telling others what is right and wrong. She had caught him staring searchingly at her a couple of times after she'd agreed with a pro-baseball team sentiment he'd expressed, but he didn't comment on it.

"It's not going to pass," Dallas said one week later. "We're not going to get the ball team."

He had marched into Julie's duplex and was pacing back and forth in her living room. He stopped to take off his jacket and throw it across the couch.

"But you raised the money, plus some. You can operate for four years, easily," Julie said.

"How could we have forgotten about the school board?" he muttered more to himself than to Julie.

"Forget about them? I thought you were on the agenda for Thursday's meeting, two weeks earlier than you'd anticipated."

"We are. But we concentrated on getting the money, not on convincing the school board that we needed the team." He stopped his pacing and faced her.

"Wade and I just went down the list, and we aren't going to get the team. Four of them oppose it."

"Are you sure?"

"We've not canvassed each member, but general opinion is that it won't pass. We think three support us. The other three are against us. Split down the middle," he said and gestured with his hands. "So the school board president will vote, and she told Wade that we don't need that team."

"You're not defeated yet. Talk to them, persuade them. You can do it, Dallas. Let's draw up a list of pros and cons. No," she said, and held up her hands toward him to ward off a verbal attack. "There are cons. You're just not aware of them. If you list the reasons people are against forming a team, you'll be able to have a quick rebuttal."

Dallas took a deep breath and let it out in a loud sigh.

"Okay. But I don't understand this."

"I hate to say it, but keep an open mind," Julie said.

She put on a pot of coffee and let it brew while they sat down at the kitchen table with pencil and paper. They argued and discussed each point.

"This is nonsense. How can you say the money should be used for a science lab when we raised the money for a baseball team? There would be no money if we hadn't worked hard for it. We couldn't have convinced people to put out money for a science lab."

"I realize that, sad as it may be. I'm merely pointing out some of the objections the teachers have. The librarian wants more reference books. We could use a computer lab."

"Then let them form their own committee and raise the money. It's not an easy job," Dallas said and jumped up to pour himself another cup of coffee. "I have practically groveled to some of the businesses in town, and believe me, that wasn't easy."

"I know that, Dallas. I'm not working against you. I'm showing you the opposition. You must come up with reasonable responses to their objections."

"Okay, okay. Sorry I lost my temper." He stood up from the table, took her hand, and pulled her to her feet.

"I'm really sorry," he apologized again. "I need to get this school board off my mind for a little bit, and I know just the diversion I want."

He swung her up in his arms and carried her to the couch. He sat down still holding her tightly in his arms. His kisses landed on her cheek, on her closed eyelids, on her forehead, and finally on her lips.

Julie wound her arms around him, pulling him closer.

"Julie," he murmured as he kissed her again and again.

She kissed him back, all her emotions concentrating on her love for Dallas.

He finally pulled away and guided her head to rest on his chest. Julie could hear his heart pounding, matching the rhythm of her own.

"I think," he said and cleared his throat. "I think I'd better go while I still have some willpower left."

"You're probably right," Julie said, but made no move to get off the couch.

They held each other for several more minutes until with mute agreement they stood up and walked arm-in-arm to the door.

"Don't worry about the school board," Julie told him. "God will work things out in His own way."

"What school board?" Dallas asked and grinned.

## fifteen

The school board had decided to hold the November eighth meeting in the high school auditorium. *A power move,* Julie thought. The board sat at tables on the stage, while those attending sat in the audience, as if watching a play over which they had no control.

Usually the meetings were held in the cafeteria. Although there was a head table, there were also tables for those attending, and they were on the same level.

*Yes, it was a definite power move,* she decided. It was not a good omen for the committee.

The president of the board, a woman in her fifties, followed the usual order of business. Minutes were read; a financial report was filed for audit. Old business took an enormous amount of time.

Julie sat with Dallas and glanced around at the packed house. The committee and its supporters outnumbered the opposition by three to one, and they sat together. Many sported the red Tribune High School ball caps. The smaller group, the opponents, sat to one side. It was as if invisible ushers had asked which side they were on as the townspeople had filed in.

"Under new business, we have the first grade teachers from South Elementary presenting a grant proposal. If we approve this grant as written, it will be forwarded to the state. Mrs. Cook, you have the floor."

Mrs. Cook stepped to a microphone on the auditorium floor and talked at great length about the reading and writing grant. She sat down to loud applause from the audience.

"That's a hard act to follow," Dallas whispered to Julie.

"You can do it."

"Does anyone else wish to speak to that question?" the president asked.

No one stepped forward. A couple of board members asked questions.

"Let's vote," the president said. "A show of hands, please. All those in favor of sending this grant application on to the state level?" She counted. "All opposed? The measure passes five to one."

She consulted her agenda, although everyone in the audience knew what was coming next.

*Please God, help me through this ordeal,* Dallas prayed silently.

"Also under new business, we have the Baseball for Tribune High School Committee report. Dallas Stone."

Dallas stepped to the microphone amid loud cheers and applause. He had talked to multiple businesses and community groups during the preceding two months and had gained confidence in his speaking ability. He was surprised to find his hands weren't shaking and his voice was steady.

He told the school board about the committee's activities and the support the community had shown for a high school baseball team. After he finished, applause rang through the auditorium.

Julie nodded at Dallas when he turned to look at the audience. They had agreed that a short speech with questions to follow would be to their advantage. A couple of board members always asked questions, as if to prove to the audience that they had been listening.

"What items have you addressed?" one board member asked.

"What expenses have we foreseen?" Dallas restated the question. The board member nodded, and Julie cringed. Dallas should have started enumerating uniforms, equipment, and coaches' salaries instead of making the man look like an imbecile.

Dallas answered the question, and then took another one from a second board member. "Why do you think the money should be spent on another sport instead of on a science lab, or computers?"

Dallas had been waiting for this question. "The money was raised for a baseball program. It would be dishonest to use it for anything else. If the ball program is denied, we will refund the money to the contributors, not decide how to spend it. If the school wants a new science lab, then it should be a budget item that our taxes pay for, or they should form their own committee."

The crowd roared its approval of Dallas's response. Julie winced. Dallas should have stopped before he told them to raise the money themselves. He was not being tactful, and she was afraid the body language of the members was screaming disapproval.

"Any other questions?" the president asked. Silence. "Is there anyone who would speak to the opposite point of view?"

The high school librarian approached the microphone. "I understand Mr. Stone's position that we can't spend his committee's money any other way than on a baseball team. However, I will address a different aspect. Do we need another sport in the curriculum?

"We have basketball, football, golf, tennis, and track. Why add one more sport? It will only mean that more students will miss classes to play a game. We're in the business of educating students, not teaching them to be athletes. We already have gym classes for that." The group of teachers and their supporters cheered.

"Any questions from the board?" the president asked. The two normal questioners remained quiet this time. "How does the administration feel?" she asked the superintendent. That was normal procedure; Julie wasn't surprised at the question.

"I...uh...I support the committee and I support my teachers," the superintendent said. "As an individual, I wish we could have a baseball team. As an administrator, I should stand with my teachers."

"He's riding the fence!" Dallas whispered to Julie. "He told us he was behind us one hundred percent."

"Anyone else from the floor to speak to the question?"

Julie found herself on her feet and heading for the microphone. *Please help me say the right thing, God.* She felt Dallas's gaze boring into her back.

"I'm Julie Russell," she introduced herself to the board. "I teach junior English and American literature. From the beginning, I've been opposed to adding baseball to our sports program. But I've had a change of heart.

"I have been teaching my students about the spirit of America. Of forging ahead, exploring new vistas, and the rugged individualism that has made our country great. Of freedom of speech, freedom of religion, and freedom to pursue happiness.

"Now, I am not about to say that baseball has made our country great. But it is a part of the American dream; it's our national pastime.

"I've taught Walt Whitman's poem, 'I Hear America Singing.' Where better could you hear America singing than at baseball parks across our country as the crowd joins in the national anthem?

"I've seen America playing. One summer night I flew in a small plane across Missouri. An unearthly trail of halos led me from small town to small town to larger cities. Those halos were the circles of lights from the baseball parks. Across our country, ordinary people had gathered to enjoy a baseball game, a game of individual skill and team effort.

"The dream of those boys who play in Little League parks is to be major league players. Few will make it. But should their dream end at age fifteen? Shouldn't they be given a chance to play through high school?

"I believe we should have a baseball team at Tribune High School. No, we don't need it. We want it. Through American ingenuity and determination we have earned the money to support it. We are not asking for money, not a thin dime. We ask nothing more of the school board than approval for this American dream."

Julie stood at the microphone. The auditorium was still. As she turned to take her seat, the crowd erupted and sprang to its feet, applauding. Dallas pulled her into his arms.

"You were magnificent," he yelled to be heard over the roar of the crowd. "Magnificent."

The president beat her gavel against the table. "Order, order." The crowd ignored her for another full minute. "Order, order." Finally the crowd calmed and sat down.

"Is there anyone else to speak to the question?" No one rose. "Let's vote by a show of hands. All those in favor of allowing the committee to operate a baseball program in the high school?"

Three hands shot up. A second later a fourth hand joined them. A moment passed before a fifth hand reached into the air. Reluctantly, a sixth hand lifted.

Dallas swung Julie around as the crowd again came to its feet.

"You were wonderful," he shouted.

Tears stung Julie's eyes. She had surprised herself. It was an emotional moment for many, she concluded as she looked around. The glow on the faces of the committee members was the same as on the baseball players when they had beaten Gentry in the exhibition game.

"Order, order," the president called. She pounded her gavel again.

When the crowd quieted down the president called on the superintendent for a personnel report.

"We recommend that the board hire as baseball coach, Dallas Stone, and as assistant coach, Barney Adamson, who currently serves as assistant football coach."

Julie watched Dallas step back to talk to the principal of the high school. He whispered something, got an answer, then resumed his seat beside her.

The school board approved the hiring of the new coaches. Again the auditorium resounded with applause.

It was an hour later, after the excitement had died down, when Dallas drove Julie home. They sat on the couch rehashing the events of the evening.

"You were great, Julie. Thanks."

"Congratulations on your new job. You'll make a wonderful coach. By the way, what did you ask the principal?"

"I asked him if there was a rule against husband and wife working at the same school."

"And is there?"

"No. Julie, I don't have the persuasive powers you just showed at the school board meeting, so I'll just ask you straight out."

"You persuaded a town to back your ideas of a high school baseball team. I'd call that persuasive powers."

"Good. I love you, Julie, and with God's help, maybe I can persuade you to marry me."

"Easily," she said and beamed. "Start persuading."

# A Letter To Our Readers

Dear Reader:

In order that we might better contribute to your reading enjoyment, we would appreciate your taking a few minutes to respond to the following questions and return to:

Karen Carroll, Editor
Heartsong Presents
P.O. Box 719
Uhrichsville, Ohio 44683

1. Did you enjoy reading *Gentle Persuasion?*
   ❑ Very much. I would like to see more books by this author!
   ❑ Moderately
   ❑ I would have enjoyed it more if

   _____

2. Where did you purchase this book?_____

   _____

3. What influenced your decision to purchase this book?
   ❑ Cover            ❑ Back cover copy
   ❑ Title            ❑ Friends
   ❑ Publicity        ❑ Other

4. Please rate the following elements from 1 (poor) to 10 (superior).
   - ❏ Heroine  ❏ Plot
   - ❏ Hero  ❏ Inspirational theme
   - ❏ Setting  ❏ Secondary characters

5. What settings would you like to see in Heartsong Presents Books?

   _____

   _____

6. What are some inspirational themes you would like to see treated in future books?

   _____

   _____

7. Would you be interested in reading other Heartsong Presents books?
   - ❏ Very interested
   - ❏ Moderately interested
   - ❏ Not interested

8. Please indicate your age range:
   - ❏ Under 18  ❏ 25-34  ❏ 46-55
   - ❏ 18-24  ❏ 35-45  ❏ Over 55

Name _____

Occupation _____

Address _____

City _____ State _____ Zip _____

**HEARTS♥NG PRESENTS** books are inspirational romances in contemporary and historical settings, designed to give you an enjoyable, spirit-lifting reading experience.

*HEARTSONG PRESENTS TITLES AVAILABLE NOW:*

*ABOVE TITLES ARE $2.95 EACH*

**Send to:** Heartsong Presents Reader's Service
P.O. Box 719
Uhrichsville, Ohio 44683

Please send me the items checked above. I am enclosing
$_____ (please add $1.00 to cover postage and handling).
Send check or money order, no cash or C.O.D.s, please.
**To place a credit card order, call 1-800-847-8270.**

NAME _____

ADDRESS _____

CITY / STATE _____ ZIP_____
HPS MARCH

# HAVE YOU MISSED ANY OF THESE TITLES?

These additional titles in our Romance Reader series contain two complete romance novels for the price of one. You'll enjoy hours of great inspirational reading. Published at $7.95 each, these titles are available through Heartsong Presents for $3.97 each.